LOVE ♥ IN LAGANAS

Maria Angelides, a trainee marine biologist, plans to visit the Greek island of Zakynthos, hoping to see loggerhead turtles, monk seals — and perhaps even the Greek father she has never known . . . Professor Nikos Cristol, an important visitor to the Marine Centre, offers to fly her to the island in his company plane. Enjoying the hospitality of the Cristol family, she becomes attracted to Nikos. But, confused by his intentions, will Maria really be able to find happiness with Nikos — or discover the truth about her father?

Books by Glenis Wilson
in the Linford Romance Library:

WEB OF EVASION

GLENIS WILSON

LOVE IN LAGANAS

Complete and Unabridged

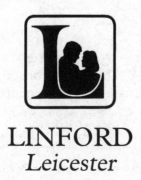

LINFORD
Leicester

First published in Great Britain in 2006

First Linford Edition
published 2007

British Library CIP Data

Wilson, Glenis
   Love in Laganas.—Large print ed.—
   Linford romance library
   1. Fathers and daughters—Fiction
   2. Zakynthos (Greece)—Fiction
   3. Love stories 4. Large type books
   I. Title
   823.9′14 [F]

   ISBN 978–1–84617–646–3

Published by
F. A. Thorpe (Publishing)
Anstey, Leicestershire

Set by Words & Graphics Ltd.
Anstey, Leicestershire
Printed and bound in Great Britain by
T. J. International Ltd., Padstow, Cornwall

This book is printed on acid-free paper

1

'Laganas? You're going on holiday to Laganas? But that's on the Greek island of — '

'Zakynthos.' Maria nodded, smiling at the expression on her friend, Sophie's face.

'Oh, oh . . . don't tell me. You can't get enough of God's aquatic little creatures working here,' she arched one arm to encompass the whole of the Marine Aquatic Centre where they both worked, 'so you're going to join the turtle volunteers.'

Sea turtles were on the endangered list and the authorities in Greece could never get enough helpers. Their newspaper always ended with a plea for more volunteers.

'I wish! Anyway, I'd hardly call a loggerhead turtle little. Weighing one hundred kilograms and measuring 85 cm is hardly small. No, you have to commit to at least four weeks or more, and since my leave won't stretch to that, I'm going as your ordinary tourist. 'Course, I'm hoping to see turtles and possibly even monk seals, if I'm really lucky.' Maria fed a sprat to Bambi, the common seal pup who was mewling plaintively and splashing in the shallow water lapping around her wellingtons.

Bambi was the youngest one of seven babies who had been rescued from the sea after being orphaned when their mothers died from the prevalent gastric virus currently decimating their numbers around the coast.

'If the present rumour's right, we shall be having two or three disabled turtles here before long. It's a busman's holiday.'

'I suppose you could say so, but I'm going for two weeks and I shall spend that being a sight-seeing tourist and go all over the island. Probably cruise round the entire coastline.'

'By yourself?' Sophie pulled a face.

'Well, judging from your reaction, I can't see anyone else from here wanting to go, can you? And I certainly don't think my mother will. So, yes, it looks like I'm on my own.'

Julia Angelides, Maria's mother, had married a Greek, but since the marriage had barely lasted a year before she'd returned home bringing the baby with her, Maria's upbringing had been traditionally British. All traces of her Greek parentage had been disowned and Maria's questions as a child quietly but firmly discouraged and left un-answered.

No, Maria thought ruefully, it wasn't something her mother would ever consider doing, albeit briefly, returning to the Ionian islands. Just what her reaction would be on hearing about the proposed trip wasn't something to dwell on.

However, Maria intended returning to the family home for the coming weekend, she'd tell her then. And not only that, she mused, there were questions to be asked, lots of them, all the ones left unasked and undisturbed during her childhood that now, as an adult, she would like answered.

This trip could prove to be a catalyst.

'Darling, oh, it's so lovely to see you,' Julia enfolded Maria in a warm hug.

'And it's great to be home. I tell you, that flat is spartan, believe me, but you don't notice until you — '

'Come face to face with palatial living?' Julia suggested smiling broadly.

Maria looked around the familiar comfortable, but shabby little house. It was filled not with priceless antiques, but with love. And that was priceless. 'I was going to say until you're met with a warm loving welcome. That place is impersonal, cold. It's certainly not home.'

'Bless you, darling.' Her mother threaded an arm through hers. 'Come on through to the kitchen. There's lasagne for lunch.'

Maria quailed inwardly. It was going to be much more difficult than she'd expected. Undoubtedly, Julia was going to be upset and it was this aspect that she shied away from. They'd supported each other from the start. Initially, of course, her mother had taken on the role of sole protector and provider throughout Maria's childhood.

As Maria grew up, their roles had subtly altered. Now, they were there for each other, their love an unbreakable bond.

Maria shivered slightly, however unpleasant, confessing to the imminent holiday had to be done — and straight away, before she let herself weaken and called off the trip. Too much was at stake.

She felt a rise of guilt because she hadn't come clean with Sophie as to the real reason behind her decision to go to Zakynthos. Nor did she intend to tell her mother. At least, not yet, until the outcome of the trip was known.

Julia placed the cafetiere, milk and mugs on a tray, and a jar of honey. Despite Maria's apprehension, the sight brought a smile to her lips.

'You're the only person who always remembers I take honey in coffee.'

'I'm your mother. It's in the job description.'

'I think I'll take two spoonfuls instead of one. I need a spine-strengthener.'

Julia, very carefully, picked up the tray before peeking over the top of her glasses at Maria. 'Like that, is it?'

'Hmmmm . . . '

'Let's go into the other room then. If I'm sitting down when you tell me . . . whatever . . . it won't matter if my knees give way.'

The lounge was a cool oasis after the warmth of the kitchen.

Julia settled herself in the wing chair. She leant back, resting an elbow on the worn green velvet, cupping her chin. 'Right, go on, surprise me.'

So Maria did.

'I'm not being deliberately awkward. Going to Zakynthos to hopefully see loggerhead turtles in the wild is something I really want to do. You do see that, Mum, don't you? You do understand?' There was a pleading for understanding behind Maria's words.

Julia, lips a thin tight line, pressed the flat of her palm hard on the coffee plunger. It served a double purpose, necessary for the coffee and with her hand held firmly down there was no chance either of Maria seeing the sudden, betraying tremble.

Always at the back of her mind, had been the possibility of Maria returning to Greece now it looked like becoming a certainty. Although, Julia clutched at the tiny hope, it was not for the reason she had dreaded.

Maria's last sentence brought to the forefront of her memory bank all the long ago years which seemed to spread out before her like a map. It had begun innocently enough, like most import sequential happenings, with Julia taking Maria to the local pet shop where they'd bought a small fishing net on a short cane.

Spring had followed late after an ice-hard winter and the pond in the triangle field at the end of the lane had been a rejoicing, vigorous explosion of aquatic life. The ubiquitous tadpoles had been there in thousands wriggling and jiggling in the murky green water. But to Julia's surprise, four-year old Maria's exclamations of delight had also been over the less obvious forms of pond-life: the water-boatmen, caddis flies and mosquito larvae. Ever after during that year, when asked where she would like to go for an outing, the answer was always, to the pond.

Although as she had grown so had her choice of venue. By the age of eight, this encompassed the aquatic and reptile exhibition in the nearby city, the koi fish farm and the Marine Life and Seal Sanctuary on the East Coast. A never flagging, endurable enthusiasm for all aspects of aquatic life. And from a childhood enthusiasm, it had grown into an adult passion.

Achieving five 'A' levels, Maria had

known at once what she wanted to read at University: Zoology. Achieving this degree would give her a firm base from which to train further.

Secretly, and oh so regretfully, she had kissed goodbye forever to their cosy twosome. Invariably, this would mean Maria being away from home. Julia had made a promise to herself she would let her go, both physically and mentally and allow her daughter to begin studying for what she most desired to be, a marine biologist.

2

Watching the strong emotions flit across her mother's face, Maria felt guilt-ridden and very uncertain. If it was this painful for her, perhaps it would be better to let the chance go by, settle for a conventional holiday and forget about going to Zakynthos. Forget all about her own past and concentrate upon the future.

'May I ask a question?' Julia raised the cafetiere and poured out two drinks.

'Please.'

'Is it a sudden decision, going to the island, or have you been considering it for quite a while?'

Maria took her coffee and trickled in a spoonful of honey. The significance of her mother's words was quite clear — Is it simply because of the sea turtles or is there a hidden agenda?

'I want to be completely honest, Mum yes, I've thought a lot about going to Greece. Up to now, my life's been so full, school, university, getting a job to fund the next stage of study, there really hasn't been any chance to go. But now . . . ' Their eyes met.

'Now you'd like to see where you started life.'

Maria seized the escape route, felt deceitful in doing so, but knowing agreement would satisfy and calm her mother's fears, squashed the feeling. 'Surely it's a natural enough thing. But truly, I'd like to see turtles in their natural habitat.'

Julia nodded. 'Oh yes, I can certainly understand that.'

'You've never said exactly where in Greece I was born.' Maria looked steadily at her mother. 'And I don't even know my father's name . . . ' The unspoken questions hung heavily in the air between them.

For a minute or two, Julia lowered her eyes and remained silent, watching the spiral of steam rising from her hot coffee.

Julia took a sip from her cup and raised her head to scrutinise her daughter. 'I think,' she began, 'since you're no longer a child and in need of protection, you have a right to know.'

'Tell me,' Maria whispered, her heart was thudding uncomfortably making it difficult to breathe. From childhood she'd desperately wanted to know and her questions had been parried leaving her confused and frustrated.

Now, after more than twenty years, she was about to be told. It seemed a momentous moment and she was suddenly very nervous.

Julia set down her cup and reached for her daughter's hand. 'His name is Leonidas, he's a marine biologist.'

'Like father, like daughter,' Maria said shakily, letting his name imprint itself in her mind. 'So, he's Leonidas Angelides. Why did you keep it secret?'

'There were reasons, valid ones, why I didn't tell you from the beginning.

There still are.' She frowned. 'You stopped asking me years ago and I suppose I thought you'd finally let it drop and would never ask me again. But,' she sighed, 'I was wrong. Now you're an adult, it's different.'

Taking a deep breath, she smiled gently, 'You were actually born on the island of Zakynthos. Ironic, isn't it?'

For the whole one hundred and thirty miles drive south back to her flat in Darrington, with her father's name indelibly imprinted forever in her brain, one word dominated Maria's thoughts, Zakynthos.

It had given her such a jolt hearing her mother say it, she was still in a state of mild shock. Ironic, Julia had called it. Maria called it destiny. She knew when she arrived back, the first place she'd go was the local library. She needed to find out as much as was possible about the island.

And there wasn't much time. She was due to fly out in less than a week.

By-passing the tiny staff canteen

adjacent to the main public restaurant at the Marine Aquatic Centre on Monday lunchtime, Maria headed for the main library only a few minutes walk away in Darrington. Disappointedly, despite scouring the computer book search, it showed there was very little published about the island. Selecting the only book actually on the library shelf, she went to find the nearest restaurant.

The biggest and most popular one, Darrington being a seaside town, it was packed with office workers, and normal shoppers together with a hefty sprinkling of tourists and trippers. Maria checked her watch, she had only twenty minutes left before she was due back at work.

Finally, with the book thrust under one arm and carrying a tray with coffee and a pastry oozing cream and calories, she walked between the tables.

Just as she reached the final row of tables, a mini-skirted young woman, pushed away her empty cup and stood up. She smiled and gestured to Maria. 'This one's free now.'

'Great, thanks a lot.' Maria dumped the tray and slid into the seat. The book on Zakynthos slipped from beneath her arm and plopped heavily on to the table, slithered along and bumped against the cup and saucer belonging to the other person seated at the table.

Seeing the missile coming, he thrust out a hand and retrieved the book as a little of his coffee slopped over on to the table. Lifting it out of harm's way, he automatically scanned the title. Lifting dark, seductive eyes, he regarded Maria closely. 'You are going to visit this . . . place?'

Filled with embarrassment, Maria nodded. 'I'm sorry it nearly upset your drink.'

He waved a dismissive hand. 'Please, it's of no consequence.'

He was looking at her now with undisguised interest. Maria felt a thrill of excitement tingle through her. He was a most attractive man, handsome in the way only darkly-tanned Mediterranean men were. His crisply curling black hair was worn perhaps a shade too long for it brushed against the collar of his immaculate white shirt.

There was a twinkle of merriment now in those dark compelling eyes. 'Are you not going to tell me?'

'Pardon?' Maria realised she had been staring and felt herself redden. He tapped the cover of the book lightly with a fingernail.

'Oh, yes, I see.' Attempting to get a grip, she took a sip of hot coffee. 'I am actually.'

'Hmmm. It could be interesting.'

'I'm hoping it will be. I've never been before.'

'Can I ask whether it is business or pleasure, a holiday perhaps?'

'No, well, not exactly.' She began to nibble the cream cake whilst he finished off the remains of his drink. On the point of telling him she was going over to look for turtles, the words stuck in her throat as she recalled Sophie's reaction — and that was from a committed animal lover.

The man was watching her, waiting with interest to hear what she was going to say.

'It's somewhere I've always wanted to go,' she finished lamely.

'And so now at last, you are realising your dream.' He smiled at her.

Their eyes met, and held. Maria felt a frisson of pleasurable excitement. She'd never before felt so instantly attracted to any man. What a pity they'd no time to get to know each other better. When she left the restaurant she'd never see him again.

Nodding towards the book, she said, 'I intend to spend the evening reading up about the island.'

'They have a magic all their own, the islands,' he went on softly, a little dreamily. 'Once you have been you will understand and you will want to go again.'

'Oh, I doubt it. This will be a once only visit, I'm afraid.'

'That is very sad. You should not deny yourself pleasurable experiences.'

Maria finished the delicious pastry and gulped. She dare not look directly at him. His words were no doubt entirely innocent, but she felt the telltale burn on her cheeks and knew they had reddened. Coming from anyone else, the remark would not have held such a sensual double meaning but with the powerful pull of attraction she was feeling, this was dangerous ground.

She hurriedly drained her coffee. It would be much safer to leave now before she said anything stupid or compromising. 'I'm afraid I have to return to work.'

He was on his feet instantly. 'I have also finished.'

Maria smiled tightly, feeling a sudden apprehension. 'It was nice to have met you,' she said firmly and held out her hand. Even he must see this was a firm goodbye.

He took her hand but instead of shaking it, pressed her fingers to his lips. 'It passed a delightful few minutes,' he murmured as he reluctantly released her hand.

The touch of his lips had sent the blood rushing hotly through her and Maria had to steel herself not to snatch her hand away. Was it just his innate good manners that had prompted him, or did he perhaps find her attractive, too?

Hurriedly gathering up her shoulder-bag and library book in confusion, she left the restaurant. But he was obviously going in the same direction and within seconds, his long strides had reduced the distance between them and she found him walking beside her.

'Perhaps you would permit me to accompany you as we seem to be going in the same direction.'

Her pulse quickened. She knew nothing about him, not even his name. But it wasn't as though he was a disreputable layabout. The way his dark suit fitted superbly across those broad shoulders and snugly encased his narrow hips spoke volumes about his tailor and the purchase price.

'Why not.' The Marine Centre was only minutes away. Just what was she afraid of? Was it the man himself, or her emotional reaction to him?

'Unfortunately, I am only going a short way. I have a meeting in . . . ' he shot his cuff and checked the time on his gold Rolex, 'less than ten minutes. I arrived far too early. I'd allowed for the traffic being heavy, but it actually proved an easy drive down from Yorkshire.'

'That's a long drive.'

'Yes, I suppose it is. I have relatives in Malton. However, because I was far too early, I thought it best to park up and go for a coffee. I'm so glad I did.' He looked sideways at her. The twinkle in his warm dark eyes was most disconcerting.

Struggling to stay calm and in control, she said, 'You're here on business, then?'

'You could say so, although it's really

a pooling of ideas and knowledge.' He stopped walking and thrust out a hand. 'I'm so sorry, you don't even know my name, do you? Let's do things properly. I'm Nikos.' He pumped her hand enthusiastically.

'I'm Maria.'

'Aah, a beautiful name for a beautiful woman.' His eyes were now speaking an expressive age-old language to her. She had wondered earlier if he found her attractive, now she had her answer.

They resumed walking and a few moments later arrived at the road junction leading to the Marine Centre. She turned and found that he also was taking the same road. 'I'm going in here.' She pointed ahead to the wide entrance gates.

'So am I.' He looked surprised. 'Now that's a coincidence. Do you work here then?'

'Yes. My boss is Mr Broadhead, the owner.'

'Really?' He grinned. 'Now that is a coincidence. My meeting is with the same gentleman.'

It was Maria's turn to look taken aback. 'The only person he's expecting is a marine biologist, a professor Cristol.'

His grin widened. 'You're looking at him. I am Nikos Cristol.'

3

Maria tapped lightly on the mahogany door. 'Come in,' invited a male voice.

Nikos waved a hand to allow her to enter first. Feeling self-conscious at introducing the famous man to her boss, she immediately stood to one side and said, 'Professor Cristol is here, Mr Broadhead.'

The dapper lithe man behind the desk jumped to his feet and hurried forward. 'How very pleasant to meet you in person, Professor. It's so good of you to spare us some of your valuable time.'

'The pleasure is all mine, I do assure you,' said Nikos shaking the proffered hand.

In anticipation, Maria hastily went to the desk and drew up a further chair for the visitor.

Jim Broadhead looked across at her.

'Refreshments would be nice, if you please, Maria.' He raised one eyebrow and gave a very slight yet expressive tilt of his head. 'And make it for four.'

'Of course.' Maria smiled at them both and thankfully escaped. Closing the heavy office door behind her, she leaned against it with a gasp of relief. What an amazing thing to have happened. If the Professor's reputation was not actually spoken of with awe at the Marine Centre, it certainly was with deep respect, especially for his celebrated work in connection with endangered marine species, particularly monk seals.

Nikos might have spoken of his pleasure in coming, but Maria knew a visit from a man of his standing was an honour for the Marine Centre. But one raised eyebrow could convey a lot of meaning. She had to alert Alan and Neil, the two executive assistants that the famous visitor had arrived and their presence was required a.s.a.p. in the boss's office.

Ten minutes later, complete with a

spread of delicious goodies that reminded her all she'd had for lunch was a cream cake, Maria angled the tray through the door and laid it carefully on the desk. Her boss simply nodded an acknowledgement as he and the Professor were poring over a ground plan of the Marine Centre.

But just as she was closing the door, Nikos shot her a swift, brilliant smile. Even from across the far side of the room, it conveyed the equivalent of a high-voltage charge of electricity and had the effect of reducing her knees to cotton wool.

'If he's as hunky as he sounds,' said Sophie later, as they were busy scrubbing algae-coated aquariums in the utilities, 'he's bound to be married or at least has a partner.'

'He doesn't look married . . . ' Maria murmured thoughtfully.

'Oh come on! He's bound to have been snapped up years ago. How old do you think he is?'

'Probably mid-thirties.'

'No grey hairs yet, then.' Sophie

grinned wickedly.

'I didn't get that close,' Maria protested.

'A dishy man, with good manners, and you blow a fantastic chance to get a date.' Sophie shook her head in mock despair. 'Tell you what, if you don't fancy him, just introduce him to me.'

'Did I say I didn't fancy him?' Maria nonchalantly sluiced out an aquarium.

'Hey, hey!' carolled Sophie. 'So you do fancy him. And you a committed career girl.'

'Give over.' Maria stripped off her rubber gloves.

'You do, don't you?'

'OK, we're talking truth here, yes, I do. Any woman worthy to be one would drool over him. You wait, you haven't seen anything yet. When you know what he's like . . . '

'Ooh, can't wait.'

'And I can't wait to get a cup of tea. I missed lunch, well, practically.'

'Oh yes, you were going to the

library. Did you get a book on Zakynthos?'

'Just the one in stock. I shall devour it tonight.' They walked companionably in the direction of the staff canteen.

The huge ornate clock that was also a water fountain in the middle of the main courtyard struck four o'clock. Water cascaded down as the sonorous notes pealed out. It was the signal for a last-minute rush for a place by the safety rails surrounding the seal pool. The people weren't the only ones getting excited. In the pool itself, the water boiled and sprayed as a dozen large hungry seals thrashed and dived.

Peeping through the food preparation room window, Maria tugged on Wellington boots ready for the onslaught. 'Quite a crowd this afternoon. Loads of kiddies . . . oh — '

'What's the matter?' Sophie swung the handle of the rubber bucket filled with fish pieces.

Maria gripped her friend's arm. 'He's

there, in the crowd.' Sophie took a quick look.

'I can see Mr Broadhead, wait . . . yes, there's another man with him. Dark, tanned . . . and oh, wow! Is that the Professor?'

'Hmmm . . . I did warn you.'

'I don't know how I'm going to concentrate on feeding now. It's unfair of any man to be that dishy,' Sophie wailed, desperately running fingers through her mass of wild curls.

'Come on,' Maria grinned and picked up her own feeding bucket. 'It isn't us he's going to be looking at, it's the seals.'

They walked out and through on to the raised concrete above the waterline.

There was a rush as the seals, spotting them, drove through the foaming water like torpedoes and slithered part-way up the wet slope, honking in excitement.

A roar went up from the crowd ringing the pool as the big animals gulped down the fishes being thrown to them. Contrary to Sophie's prediction, both girls were fully focussed on the job of making sure each seal received its rightful allocation of fish.

It was not only a feeding session, but also an excellent opportunity to observe the individual seals close-up for any signs of injuries or changes of behaviour that could indicate the onset of illness.

But when the last piece of fish had been thrown, the seals had very reluctantly rolled and slithered their way back into the now calm water and the appreciative thunderous roar of applause was dying away, they both cast a glance towards the two men. Their boss was all smiles and the Professor was still clapping.

'I know you saw him first,' Sophie began as, back in the preparation room, they swilled out the empty buckets, 'and I wouldn't dream of cutting in, but if you don't want him . . . '

'Get real, Sophie, a man like that wouldn't look at us.'

'He might,' she said mutinously.

Before Maria could reply, there was a tap on the door and Mr Broadhead popped his head round. 'Don't let us interrupt,' he said, 'but when you've finished here could you come along to my office please, Maria? The Professor would like a word with you.'

Her thoughts squirreled round. She couldn't think where she might have fallen down on the job. The work meant far too much to her. She tried to read his face, but could detect no signs of irritation, if anything he seemed relaxed and affable. However, you weren't usually told to report to the office unless it was for a reprimand . . .

'Yes, of course,' she replied.

'Very good, carry on.' He gave a quick nod and the door closed behind him.

A few minutes later, Maria, divested of her protective uniform and rubber boots, knocked tentatively on the boss's door. Going in she found both men smiling. Her apprehension melted away as she realised this summons wasn't because of any problem with her work or presentation. But if it wasn't to do with work, she had no idea what it could be for.

'Maria,' Mr Broadhead came forward, 'Professor Cristol has decided to stay overnight and drive back to Yorkshire tomorrow. Are you busy this evening, or could you accompany him for dinner at his hotel? I, myself have an engagement, I'm afraid. My loss,' he pulled a rueful face.

Put like that, Maria knew there was no way of ducking out. It wasn't so much an invitation as an order.

And she'd already told Nikos she was staying in to read the book on Zakynthos.

'Please,' Nikos, seeing her hesitation, tilted his head and assumed a little boy lost expression, 'I'd be charmed if you would say yes. I promise I won't talk *shop* and bore you rigid.'

Her heart did skip. He was dangerously attractive, dangerous being the operative word, but she could hardly plead a headache. And she cringed at what Sophie would say about her having dinner alone with Nikos in his hotel.

Then, seeing Nikos waiting for her reply, and catching sight of that seductive, dancing twinkle lurking in his eyes, she shocked herself by saying impulsively, 'I'd love to.'

4

The taxi dropped Maria outside the Granton Hall Hotel at five to eight. Nikos had insisted on sending transport. 'Since you're coming to meet me, when I should have called to collect you, it's the only way you'll ease my conscience.' Put like that there was no arguing. Again, she experienced the sensation of being swept along by a strong current.

Before she could play safe and disappear through the main doors, Nikos stepped out of the lift just a few steps from her. He had obviously been watching for the taxi to arrive. He smiled, showing perfect, white teeth.

'Maria.' Taking her hand he brushed his lips gently against her fingers. 'You're looking particularly beautiful tonight.' His words were emphasised by the appreciative warmth in those dark

33

eyes. 'Come.' He led the way into the restaurant and drew out a chair for her.

'Thanks.' She sat down. Nikos was wearing the same suit, but had changed into a clean, crisp shirt and tie. She caught a faint whiff of fresh, tangy aftershave.

'I thought perhaps you might like to choose.' He handed her a menu.

She ran her eyes down the tempting dishes on offer. 'Soup, please . . . and spinach cannelloni.'

He caught the waiter's eye and ordered soup for starters and chose noisette of lamb for himself.

Maria declined his offer of wine, preferring instead to pour a glass of still mineral water. 'You said you have relations here in England?'

'That's right, on my mother's side. Actually, it's my grandmother. She has lived here for many years now. My grandfather ran a chain of fish and chip shops.' The corner of his mouth quirked up a little. 'I suppose that must sound strange to an English person. I mean, it's supposed to be your traditional fast food dish, isn't it?'

'An awful lot of our fish and chip shops seem to be owned by Greeks.' Maria sipped chilled water. 'I think you must be a very industrious nation.'

'Ah, no, no. Now that is where you are quite wrong. Really, we are the laziest people. It is our, what do you say, laid-back, way of life? Could be something to do with all that heat. From two until around five every afternoon we have our siesta. Far too hot to work. Then of course we are all refreshed later and everybody goes out at six o'clock for our volta.'

Maria wrinkled her nose a little. 'You've lost me.'

'Put simply, it's a walk, everybody goes out. It has been a long-standing custom.'

The soup arrived. The waiter set it down carefully in front of Maria causing the candle floating in its surrounding rose petals to flicker madly, sending little slivers of silver light dancing across the cutlery.

They ate in a snug, companionable silence and, warmed both by the soup and his presence, Maria felt a bubble of happiness rise inside. Nikos was a personable, charming man, blatantly a ladies-man — his charisma and sex appeal drew admiring glances from several other women in the dining room, but for tonight at least, he was her escort. He made her feel very much a desirable woman.

Undoubtedly, when he returned to Yorkshire, she would never see him again, but whilst this evening lasted, she would enjoy it to the full. It was probably a good thing she would only have this one date — and really it wasn't even that, having been fixed up by her boss, because Nikos was the type of man with whom it would be so easy to fall in love. She pushed the thought firmly away.

He was way, way out of her league and it was pure fluke she was sharing a table with him tonight. As far as she knew he might even be married. But certainly with those good looks and air of supreme self-confidence he was bound to have a girlfriend.

'You have a boyfriend?'

With a start, Maria gathered herself. It was almost as though his thoughts had run parallel to her own. 'No, no-one.'

'Oh, come.' He leaned forward and gazed at her. 'Someone as pretty as yourself, it follows naturally.'

'I'm sorry I must disappoint you. There is no-one, truly. My work comes first . . . and last.'

He nodded, serious now. 'Yes, that I can understand. My work also is of tremendous importance to me. It leaves little time to devote to women. And a woman should have time spent on her. That is, if one is serious about her, of course. Time is so much more valuable than money.'

'Speaking as a female, I agree. But I'm sure most men wouldn't.'

'Then they do not know how to treat

a woman properly. And if their marriage fails . . . ' He spread his hands. 'It is entirely their fault.'

'Well, I certainly don't intend to get married for a very long time.'

'And why is that?'

'I'd like to study. At the moment I'm taking time to earn some money specifically for that. But since it's in the same line of work, I'm not wasting time.'

'Most commendable. And what is it you'll be studying?'

Maria coloured. 'Marine biology.'

'Aaah . . . my own field of work.'

The conversation flowed along on general topics and there were no awkward moments of stilted silence and the evening passed enjoyably. Maria was relaxed and enjoying herself and it was with acute disappointment she realised they'd actually finished coffee and the evening was almost ended.

'And you're going back to Yorkshire tomorrow, aren't you?'

'Yes. I rejoin my brother for three

more days at Grandmother's house and then we fly back.'

'That's Friday. I'm flying then, too.'

'Ah, yes. Your book in the café, the one you should have been reading tonight.' His eyes twinkled.

'Hmm.' She laughed. 'I shall read it tomorrow night instead.'

'And you are going to Zakynthos, yes?'

'That's right.'

'May I ask you, have you already booked an airline ticket?'

She looked across the table at him in surprise. 'No, not as yet. The flights are usually cheaper at the last moment and since I don't have a lot of money to throw about, I'm leaving buying it until the end of the week.'

'I see.' He pursed his lips. 'May I ask a question?'

'Yes . . . of course.'

'Do you trust me?'

'Well.' She flushed, looking into his dark eyes. They were not twinkling now but serious, searching. Impulsively, she aid, 'Yes, yes, I think so.'

'Good.' He smiled. 'Then, may I offer you a seat in my plane?'

Maria gasped. 'I beg your pardon?'

'My brother, George, he is a qualified pilot. We have a Lear jet parked at a private airstrip near Malton.'

She stared at him in shocked surprise. 'Your own private plane?' she managed to whisper.

'It's not mine personally, you understand. It belongs to my father, the company's plane. But we use it when we need to. I don't fly myself but, as I said, George does.'

'And you're offering me a flight to Zakynthos?'

'If you would like to be my guest, yes.'

'But where are you going, what's your destination?'

He threw back his head and laughed. 'What a woman for questions. Would you believe, Zakynthos?'

For a second the room rocked. 'I don't know what to say,' she spluttered.

'Then, say yes. After all it will save you a great deal of money which you can put away in your training fund.'

Maria was tempted. 'But where will I meet you? If you're going to Yorkshire tomorrow . . . '

'No worries. George will fly us down on Friday and find a landing strip near here. I'll ring you at the Marine Centre and fix the details.'

She nodded, overwhelmed by the thought of actually going to the place she'd longed to see for so many years and not only that, but also travelling there in style — by private plane.

★ ★ ★

'You are joking, you have to be.' Sophie, eyes wide with disbelief, dropped her ballpoint and clutched Maria's arm. 'Tell me it's a wind-up.' They were in the staff office filling in the daily care charts, but work stopped immediately Sophie heard the exciting news.

'Sorry.' Maria grinned. 'It's true. I

couldn't hardly believe it either.'

'Wow! Holed up in a tiny cabin with that dishy man for — how long does the flight take?

'About four hours. We're going to a private landing strip at the side of the main runway at Zakynthos Airport. 'That's near Zakynthos town, the capital.'

'And after you've landed, what then? Will you be seeing him again, as in, for a date?'

'Very unlikely.' Maria sighed. 'I'm sure he must have a partner.'

'But you haven't asked him, have you? I should if it was me.'

I'm just so happy to be going to Zakynthos.'

'How long have you been wanting to go?'

'Ever since I was a child, except I didn't know then it was Zakynthos. All I knew was it was one of the Greek islands.'

'Right,' Sophie said slowly, looking earnestly at her friend. 'Do you want to tell me about it? Oh, I don't mean now,' she added quickly as Maria gestured towards the mound of paperwork waiting to be dealt with. 'How about you come round to mine this evening.'

Maria ran lightly up the three stone steps and pressed the doorbell later that night.

'Hi,' she greeted Sophie as the door opened.

They ate pizza off trays perched on knees. 'Hmmm . . . delicious.' Sophie pushed aside her plate and reached for a glass of wine.

'Now.' Sophie glugged an inch down her glass. 'I want to know everything that happened last night. And don't leave out the tasty bits.'

'He's taking me to Zakynthos, in their company's private plane.'

'Does he fly it himself?'

'No, apparently the pilot is George, his brother.'

'A brother, eh.' Sophie's eyes gleamed. 'And just where is this George right now?'

Maria grinned. 'Safely out of your way up in Yorkshire. Nikos has a grandmother up there at Malton.'

'Really, and did he ask about your family?'

'Not really. There's not a lot I could tell him if he did. I mean, I know there's Mum up in Radcliffe-on-Trent in Nottinghamshire, but my grandparents are dead.'

'What was your mother's maiden name?'

'Wilson. Our family is one of the oldest in the village. My great-grandfather built the house at the beginning of the twentieth century.'

'And your mum still lives in the same house, then?'

'Yes.'

'Well, that's what you call roots.'

'I guess, except . . . Oh, Sophie, I've not told anybody else ever, but now, perhaps it is time . . . '

Sophie took one look at Maria's face and reached for the wine bottle, topping up both their glasses. 'You look like you need a bit of help.'

Maria flashed her a brief, grateful smile. 'There's always been a no-go area about my roots, both parental and geographical. I only found out last weekend I was born on Zakynthos. Probably, if I hadn't told Mum about the trip, I might never have found out.'

'But what about your father?' Don't you know who he is?'

'He and Mum were married, that's why I take the name of Angelides, but I don't know anything else about him. I wish I did.'

'Then why not ask your mum?' Sophie said sympathetically.

'Because in the past it's always been taboo. I used to ask questions when I was a child, but neither my grandmother nor mum would tell me. However, Mum did let slip a couple of pieces of information. She told me my father's name is Leonidas and he's a marine biologist.'

'Really.' Sophie wriggled to the edge of her seat. 'Isn't that interesting. I mean, considering you want to study and become one, and Nikos is one, too. I say,' her voice rose in excitement, 'Do you think they know each other? You know, over there, in Zakynthos?'

Maria shook her head. 'I've no idea.'

Sophie studied her closely. 'But that's why you're going to Zakynthos, isn't it? It's not really to look for loggerhead sea turtles, is it? You're hoping to find your father.'

Maria stared back at her. 'Is it that transparent?' she whispered.

'Yes.'

Maria glanced down at her hands. They were tightly clenched, nails digging in. She unclenched them and made a deliberate attempt to relax. 'Do you think Mum has reached the same conclusion?'

Sophie thought about it. Finally, she said, 'No, no, I don't. Your mum doesn't know anything about Nikos, does she?'

Maria shook her head. 'I didn't meet

him until I came back from visiting her.'

'Therefore, she doesn't know of a possible connection with your father being a marine biologist.'

'I don't want her to know I'm looking for him. It would be bound to cause her distress if she knew.'

'But why doesn't she want you to know anything about him? Is there some dark secret? Perhaps there's something that will hurt you if you find out the truth.'

'I've never thought about that.' Maria's brow furrowed. 'I think you could be right, Sophie.'

'How do you propose to find him? I mean, you've no starting point. Are you going up to see your mum again before flying off?'

'No. But I am going to telephone, I'd already decided that. I'm going to ask her where on Zakynthos I was born. There must surely be records on the island.'

Sophie nodded. 'That's right. And if

you can find the record, it should give your father's details.'

'Well, at least I know his christian name.'

'I think you're in for a tough time, but I feel you already know that.'

'It's certainly not going to be easy,' Maria admitted, 'but I'm determined to try.'

'And it looks like fate's giving you a push with Nikos offering to take you, you know, like a meant thing.' She downed the rest of her wine. 'When do you fly?'

At her words, Maria felt a shiver of nervous excitement run down her spine. He's ringing later in the week to fix up the finer details.' She gulped the last of her own drink. 'And then — we fly out on Friday.'

5

OK, so, anything else? Maria surveyed her suitcase, small hold-all and shoulder-bag where they stood in a neat row down the hall. Passport, credit card, loose cash . . . keys, oh yes, mobile phone. She hurried to the kitchen where the phone sat on the worktop plugged into the charger.

Oh, Mum. How could she have forgotten? Hastily, she pushed the buttons. It was vital she rang to ask whereabouts on the island she'd been born. Please let Mum be in a favourable mood, Maria prayed silently. Her mother's voice answered at the third ring.

'Hi, Mum, I'm just about to leave to catch a plane,' Maria crossed her fingers and hoped her mother wouldn't ask from which airport.

'Lovely to hear from you, darling. Do

have super holiday. Have you packed suntan lotion?'

''Course, Mum. I'd so love to see the place I was born. I really can't go to Zakynthos for a first visit after all these years and not go there. Please, Mum, could you tell me where it was?' Maria held her breath and prayed some more.

Julia hesitated for a few moments and then sighed. 'Yes, yes, all right, darling. It's a natural request. And I owe it to you. The village was called Anafonitria. It's up in the northern part of the island. Your father was born there too.'

'You're a diamond! Thank you, Mum, love you to bits.'

Outside the ground floor flat a car horn sounded a double toot. 'I have to go, my . . . my car's arrived.' She felt a pang of guilt, but at least she hadn't told an outright lie and said taxi.

'Have a great time, see you when you get back.' The phone cut off.

Flinging wide the door, she raised a hand to Nikos who was sitting in the driver's seat of the black BMW, before dragging her luggage onto the pavement. He was out of the car in a second and by the time Maria had locked the front door, he'd loaded the two cases into the boot. 'You are ready?' he smiled at her.

She took a deep breath, 'Yes, all ready.'

'Then, we go.' He chivalrously opened the passenger door for her and Maria slid in.

★   ★   ★

'And this is my brother, George.'

The young man standing in the doorway of the hangar stepped forward to greet Maria. 'The pleasure is all mine,' he took her hand, smiling warmly. 'Nikos tells me you are travelling with us back to Zakynthos.'

'Yes, it's very good of you both to take me.'

'No, no, it will make the journey much more enjoyable with some female company abroad.' His smile deepened and rather reluctantly, he released her hand.

Were all Greek men this attentive and charming? Sophie ought to be here to share the experience, Maria thought. They were both dark, handsome, displaying perfect manners and above all, making her feel she was very special. The brothers were every girl's dream.

'If you would like to come aboard,' Nikos said, 'I'll just stow away your luggage. Do you need anything from the small one?' He indicated the hold-all.

'Not at all, my shoulder-bag will do just fine.'

'Right.' He hefted both cases and turned and led the way over to where the plane was waiting.

'I must go and check with the control tower,' said George, 'and then we'll be off.' He spun round and walked away across the tarmac towards the buildings.

Maria read the name painted in large letters on the side of the plane, 'Georgina. Is it named after anyone in particular?'

'Certainly is,' Nikos helped her up into the aircraft. 'The two most precious women in the world.'

'Oh?' Maria raised an eyebrow.

'My mother and sister.'

'I see.'

'My sister is actually George's twin.'

'Do you all live on Zakynthos?'

'Oh yes, our family has a large house at Lithakia, that's just up from Laganas. You could walk to the beach in a little over half an hour. Laganas itself is a very commercial resort, lots to do, lots of bars and tavernas. But where we live, it is quiet, and so very peaceful.'

'It sounds perfect,' Maria sighed with contentment, 'and you obviously love it. I can't wait to set foot on the island.'

'Aaah yes,' Nikos tilted his head to one side, 'As you told me earlier, it is your dearest wish, your dream, to visit Zakynthos, is it not?'

'Oh yes.' Looking into his liquid eyes, she found herself being drawn down into those unfathomable depths.

'Then it is an honour for me to make

your dreams come true, Maria.'

The moment of silence that followed his words was charged with unseen vibrations.

In a confusion of emotions, Maria didn't know how to reply, but simply bent her head and nodded.

'Your seat is this one, by the window,' he said briskly. 'You will be able to see Zakynthos as we come in to land.'

A delicious shiver ran right through her body. The island was calling her, she could feel it reverberating in every cell.

George came striding back and within minutes the engines began throbbing with life steadily gaining power until the aircraft quivered like a racehorse in the starting stalls. Maria peeped through the window as with a final deep roar, the aircraft sped forward down the landing strip, gaining speed all the time until the ground suddenly fell away and they were airborne.

Maria expelled a breath she hadn't

been aware she was holding and relaxed back in her seat. They were on their way, and in about four hours from now, she would be getting her first sight of the place where she'd been born. 'If you look through the window, Maria, Zakynthos is coming up ahead.' Nikos, one hand resting on the back of her seat, was leaning over her pointing.

Suddenly, her palms were sticky and although it was a smooth flight free from turbulence, she felt sick and . . . yes, also a little afraid. Of what she couldn't say. Could it be this trip was a terrible mistake? Supposing she found her father and discovered the secret of why her mother had refused to tell her anything about him, what then? It had to be something unpleasant, emotionally hurtful at the very least. But what was worse, she might find him and he reject her.

'You're not looking,' Nikos chided softly. His face was only inches from hers. 'Don't you want to see your dream?'

She glanced up at him and quickly looked away again. The magnetism of this man was an almost tangible force. It couldn't just be her. But it would be stupid to think there wasn't a girlfriend waiting for him on Zakynthos.

Taking a deep breath, she leaned forward and gazed out of the window. The surrounding sea was a shimmering aqua-marine and the island itself, rushing up to greet them now, breath-takingly beautiful.

'That is the Vassilikos Peninsula. Whenever I see it, I know I'm home.' The timbre of his voice was deeper now, warmly husky. 'There is nowhere else on earth I would rather live.'

The aircraft was losing height now. She could see olive groves flashing by beneath them and all fears and anxiety left her. Like Nikos, right now there was nowhere else she wanted to be but here.

In contrast to the lushness of the olive groves, the area around Zakynthos Airport was arid and dusty. George expertly took the plane in and landed on the private airstrip behind the main runways. He taxied to a halt.

Nikos operated the door that hinged upwards and in turn, allowed the folding steps to be lowered into place. He grinned at her, 'Come on, you must be the first to step on to Zakynthos soil.'

A light touch on her arm by Nikos reminded Maria that officialdom awaited before she could be free to enjoy her visit. But once cleared, they passed through the exit door and George raised a hand in greeting. Turning quickly to Maria, he said, 'Georgina's brought the car to meet us.'

'But I must go and find my accommodation.'

'Later,' Nikos took her arm. 'Before you do anything else, I insist you must come to our home and have a meal. It's been a long flight. You need to relax and refresh yourself.'

'Hello.' Georgina beamed round at them all then exuberantly flung her arms around George and hugged him. 'You had a good flight?'

'Smooth and easy,' Nikos said. 'Georgina, this is Maria.'

Georgina grasped Maria's hand and pumped it enthusiastically. She was dark like the two men with a vivacious friendliness. Maria liked her instantly.

'Nikos told us on the phone it is your very first visit to our island.'

Maria realised that she was expected. 'Yes.'

'Let's hope not the last. We are biased, but it is the best place in the world.'

Maria laughed, 'I'm sure. I only wish I could stay longer and see all of it.'

'But you are here for two weeks.'

'I know.' Maria sighed, 'Actually, I would have liked to act as a sea turtle volunteer at Gerekas, but it's for a minimum of four weeks or more.'

'Aaah yes,' Nikos nodded. 'The campsite is actually a World War Two bunker. All the campsites are very basic, I'm afraid.'

'I wouldn't have minded roughing it a bit, but I should probably find it very difficult to see much of the island. And I did particularly want to visit the north end.'

'That's easily arranged. But now,' Nikos said firmly, 'let's drive home. There's a meal waiting for us.'

Georgina turned right towards Lithakia. The car followed the winding road up to the village, but before Maria had chance to take very much in, Georgina turned off sharply on the left and then left again. She was driving now through olive groves that had Maria drawing in breath sharply at the beauty of the trees. She could have sat contentedly drinking in the wonderful setting, but soon the car began to slow down and a long, low house was soon visible through the trees.

Georgina deftly swung the big car in a semicircle and pulled up outside the front door. She pressed a thumb on the horn and flashed a wide smile at Maria. 'Family custom. That way Mama knows it's one of the family.' the door opened and framed a thickset man who looked exactly like an older version of Nikos.

'Hello.' He spread wide his arms to encompass them all.

'Dad, this is Maria, my business acquaintance from England.'

Maria's hand was pumped with enthusiasm. 'Welcome to Zakynthos. Nikos tells us you have never been before.'

Maria nodded. 'That's right. And I'm so pleased to be here at last. From what I've seen so far, it's outstripping my dreams.'

Mr Cristol beamed at her. 'We love our island. But come, you must meet my wife.' He led the way along the wide hall to magnificently proportioned sitting-room that seemed to take up the width of the house.

A slender, almost frail-looking, woman rose from a chair to greet them. Nikos hugged her massively.

'Mama, you are all right, yes?'

'I'm fine.' She smiled up at her eldest

son, almost swallowed up in his embrace. 'And you have brought us a guest.' Her gaze lingered on Maria. 'You are a very beautiful young woman.'

Embarrassed by the candid comment, Maria felt herself blushing.

'Yes,' Mr Cristol nodded agreement, 'truly, how do you say? An English Rose.'

'Not entirely,' Maria sought to stem the compliments. 'I'm actually half-Greek.'

'What?' Nikos stared in amazement at her. 'You never told me that.'

'Hmmm, my father is Greek.'

'No wonder you felt drawn to visit.' Georgina said.

There was a light tap on the door and a middle-aged woman popped her head round. 'Dinner is ready, sir.'

'Thank you, Jeno. We will be through in a few minutes.'

'Right,' Georgina held out her hand. 'I'm sure you'd like to freshen-up, Maria. Come on, I'll show you where the bathroom is.'

The meal was delicious, fresh monkfish and vegetables, a variety Maria had never tried before, and there was Retsina wine to drink.

'Where are you staying?' Georgina asked.

'At the self-catering apartments on Nephrine Road in Laganas.

'Ha, yes,' Mr Cristol sipped his wine. 'They're owned by a colleague of mine. He has many available on mainland Greece also. Our family is not in competition, you understand, our business interest lies in the hotel trade.'

'I see. But Nikos, he's a marine biologist.' She glanced questioningly across the table at him.

'He is also a partner,' Mr Cristol chuckled. 'You do not get to be very rich I think, as a saver of sea-life. However, it is commendable and what he wishes to do.'

Amused, Nikos said wryly, 'Thank you, Dad.'

There was a ripple of laughter round the table.

'Are you going to be very comfortable staying in self-catering?' Nikos asked her. 'I'd have thought you'd be better in a hotel.'

'They are expensive, but I expect I shall manage very well.'

'You'll be on your own, though,' Georgina said.

'I'll be fine. It isn't simply a tourist type holiday. I'm hoping to get a look at some loggerhead sea turtles, maybe if I'm very lucky, monk seals, too.'

'You would be sure to see some turtles on our friend's beach.' Mrs Cristol had been picking sparingly at her fish, but listening with interest to the conversation. 'His house is built on land which runs down to the beach south-west of here.'

'And you think he might allow me access?'

'Surely.' Nikos refilled first Maria's wineglass and then his own. 'Vassilis is an old friend of ours. His land adjoins our own.'

'That would be great. You've all been

so kind to me. I'm very grateful.'

'Not at all.' George smiled at her down the table.

'Mama and Dad are going away for a week's holiday from tomorrow,' Georgina said. 'So I'll be the one needing company. What with my boyfriend, Alex, away working on the mainland I shall be stuck here on my own.'

'You will be busy, my girl,' Costas Cristol chuckled, 'with a wedding very soon, there is plenty to keep you occupied.'

'Sounds like I should say congratulations.' Maria smiled at her. 'Is he a local man?'

'Ah yes, ours is an arranged marriage.'

Maria was taken aback. 'I had no idea they were still arranged.'

Lifting her chin, Mrs Cristol said proudly, 'We have very old established customs. Since Georgina's fifteenth birthday, she has been in an arranged marriage.'

Georgina nodded, 'Seven years. We

began our courtship about two years ago. We were chaperoned to start with, but not now.'

'Times change.' Mrs Cristol frowned. 'It used not to be allowed but . . . ' she shrugged thin shoulders.

'We must bend,' said Costas gently, 'like the olive trees before the strong wind.' He laid down his fork and reached for her hand, stroking it tenderly. 'And in two weeks our daughter will be a married woman and all will be well. She will be taken care of.'

Maria watched the play of emotion on his face. Concern for his wife's difficulty in her acceptance of modern day life, relief for Georgina's secure future and . . . something else? With a slight unease, she realised it was sadness. Now why? Perhaps if she had not been watching his expression so clearly it would have gone unnoticed for the tenor of his voice didn't alter.

No-one else appeared aware of his hidden distress. But as an outsider she saw what they, in their familiarity, did not. There was definitely something wrong. She found it quite disturbing.

However, Georgina was gaily chattering on about her wedding plans and obviously she had no idea that everything wasn't quite what it appeared.

Maria determinedly shook off the unease. It was none of her business. 'Where are you going on holiday?' she asked Mrs Cristol. 'It's so beautiful here, if I actually lived on Zakynthos, I don't think I'd want to go anywhere else.'

There was no hint of sadness in Mr Cristol's face now. He was beaming at her. 'It's our wedding anniversary, thirty-eight years in two days time. We are taking a cruise. Just a short one, mind, because of Georgina's wedding.'

'We went on our twentieth anniversary and again on our thirtieth. I loved it so much my dear husband has booked again.'

'I'm sure you'll enjoy it this time, too, Mama.' Nikos said. 'And when you come back, there will be the wedding to look forward to.' Sensitive now to the nuances around the table, Maria picked up the so slight edge of anxiety behind his words. He, too, was concealing something.

'I know,' his mother nodded her head, 'but when will your wedding be? That is something I would like to know.'

'My work comes first, you know that. I shall marry when the time is right.'

'Tsk! That is no answer at all.'

Jeno had already served dessert when Georgina, remembering the conversation before dinner, said, 'Maria, you were telling us that you're actually half-Greek. Do your parents live over in England?'

'My mother does, yes.'

'And your father?'

'Georgina,' Mrs Cristol chided. 'Maria is our guest. She is not here to be quizzed.' She tried, delicately, to conceal a yawn.

'Yes, of course, sorry.'

'I think,' Mr Cristol looked at his

watch, 'perhaps we should retire, my love. Let these young ones enjoy the rest of the evening by themselves.'

'I should be going myself,' Maria drained her coffee and placed her napkin on the snowy tablecloth.

'Please, there is no need,' the older woman placed a thin restraining hand on Maria's arm.

'Thank you, but really, I must go. I need to check out my accommodation.'

'In which case, if you would allow me,' Nikos said, 'I shall drive you over.'

'Oh, I couldn't. I'll ring a taxi.'

'No way. I couldn't possibly allow a guest to do that,' Nikos said firmly. 'Your case is still in the back of Georgina's car. I'll fish it out, put it in mine. Wait here, I'll give you a toot.'

'And you simply must come again,' George said and surprised her with a quick hug. 'We've enjoyed your company.'

'If you get stuck for company during the day, don't forget I'm here on my own,' Georgina said. 'And I hate being by myself.'

'I'll remember. And say thanks to your mum and dad before they set sail. I hope they have a wonderful wedding anniversary.'

There was a discreet pip outside. Maria stood up, 'Must go, my taxi . . . bye.'

Nikos drove competently and swiftly into Laganas and pulled up outside the holiday apartments. He turned in his seat to face her and she was acutely aware of his nearness. 'Did you enjoy our company tonight?'

'Yes, I'm very glad I accepted your invite. It's made a lovely start to my holiday.'

'Perhaps you would let me make tomorrow evening a little bit special, too. I'd like to take you out to dinner.'

'Oh.' Up until now she had not considered them to be a couple. True, they had shared dinner, but only because her boss had decreed it. Tonight it seemed she'd been invited through courtesy. But now, Nikos was acutely asking her for a date.

Maria smiled. 'I didn't expect you to ask me out. I came to Zakynthos strictly for a holiday and to see the turtles in their natural habitat, if possible.' For some reason, she withheld telling Nikos about her driving desire to find her father. 'I don't want to monopolise your time.'

'My time is my own. And I wish to spend some of it with you.' He gazed at her, waiting for an answer.

In desperation, she said, 'But don't you have a girlfriend? Your mother said something about you getting married. She sounded as though she was looking forward to it, as if you already had a girlfriend. Do you?'

A guarded look veiled his dark eyes. 'Yes, I have many friends, some of them girls.'

'I wouldn't want to cause any ill-feeling.'

'You wouldn't.' he said brusquely. 'Please, Maria, have dinner with me tomorrow. You do want to, don't you?'

She looked into those enigmatic eyes and knew she was both afraid of where this might lead and yet desperately wanted to see him again. 'OK,' she said unsteadily, 'tomorrow then.'

A smile of triumph curved his lips. 'I shall call to pick you up at eight o'clock.' He swung his long legs from the car and plucked her suitcase from the boot. Together they walked up the steps to the holiday lets.

A notice was pinned to the centre of the front door. Maria read it. 'Oh no! There's been a water pipe burst earlier today.'

Nikos bent and read the notice. 'Hmmm. The flats are temporarily uninhabitable. It seems you have to be relocated in Zakynthos itself.'

He took her arm and led her back to the car.

'Where are we going?'

'I'm taking you back with me, to Lithakia.'

'I can't possibly impose on your

71

parents,' Maria gasped.

He pushed her gently into the passenger seat and went round and slid in behind the wheel. 'Exactly what I'm saying right now.' he reached for her hand and squeezed it gently. 'Maria, it's my pleasure to have you stay as our houseguest.'

6

'But how wonderful!' Georgina's delight lit up her face. 'You see, I told you we'd love to have your company.'

'Just for tonight then,' Maria acquiesced, 'and thanks. But tomorrow, I must go to Zakynthos.'

'Why must?' George shook his head. 'There is no must. We have plenty of room. It's common sense.'

But sense wasn't the right word thought Maria, quite the opposite. Foolish would be far more appropriate. It had certainly been foolish of her to allow Nikos to railroad her into returning.

For tonight, however, she'd go along with his wishes. Already it was getting late, getting dark, it would be stupid to go dashing off across to the other side of the island. But Nikos' next words sent a quiver of nervousness down her spine.

'Staying here is the perfect base you have to admit, Maria. We're hardly any distance from Laganas and from here it's a direct route up the backbone of the island to the north. You did say you wanted to go there?' She nodded. 'Not only that,' he went on cheerfully, 'we can get you access to the beach below through our friend's estate. It's ideal to do a turtle watch from there.'

'Sorted,' George smiled at her. 'And I'd be pleased to join you on the turtle expedition.' He pushed his brother's shoulder. 'This one's far too busy seal spotting to give you the attention you deserve. Definitely, I'm your man.'

Maria covertly glanced sideways at Nikos and saw his face darken. 'Ignore this peasant,' he rapped. 'He can look elsewhere.'

For a few seconds the atmosphere became uncomfortably tense. Then Georgina came to the rescue. 'Now you two can stop it. Maria will be going places with me. Isn't that so, Maria?'

Thankfully, Maria grasped the life-belt thrown to her and nodded. 'I'm sure you two men are both far too busy to waste time escorting me around.'

Nikos looked a little hurt by her dismissal. 'Let me be the judge of that. Remember what I asked you earlier, in the car?'

Knowing she'd seem ungrateful, Maria hastened to reassure him. 'I did agree to dinner tomorrow and yes, of course, that still stands.' A slow smile curved the corners of his lips and his gaze slid across to George.

But George did not appear put out. 'By the time Maria has lunched with me earlier, she'll have no appetite left for you, big brother. You will have lunch with me, won't you, Maria?'

Maria couldn't help laughing. 'But not tomorrow. I shall go back home to England two sizes bigger at this rate.'

'I take that as a yes,' George said happily. 'Sunday it is.'

'You two, you're like kids,' Georgina frowned. 'Stop pestering her. Between you, you will drive her away.'

She turned to Maria. 'Tomorrow I say we go girlie shopping and leave these two nuisances behind. Now, come on, I'll show you your room, it's quiet and peaceful and has a very comfortable bed.'

'Sounds like heaven, I'm absolutely bushed.'

'He really fancies you, you know,' Georgina said. The two girls were walking slowly through Solomos Square in Zakynthos town, revelling in the hot morning sunshine. Maria had found it necessary to dive into one of the local shops and buy a sun-hat to protect her head. Now, confronted by Georgina's words, she tugged at the wide brim and used it as a fan. It obscured her face beautifully.

'Nikos, you mean?' She tried to sound nonchalant.

Georgina scoffed. 'Pssh, no, of course not.'

Keen disappointment flooded through Maria.

'I mean George. Don't tell me you haven't noticed he's attracted to you.' She waved a languid hand, 'A woman always knows these things.'

'I hadn't noticed.'

Georgina stopped walking and frowned. 'But you must have done. It is obvious.'

'Not to me,' Maria said firmly. She walked on towards the tall stone plinth surrounded by its protective short railings on top of which stood the statue of Dionysios Solomos.

Georgina caught her up and together they stood looking up at the impressive statue. 'Dionysios, our patron saint, was a parish priest here way back in the sixteenth century. He spent the last year of his life at the Monastery in Anafonitria.'

Maria felt her heart lurch. 'That's in the north of the island. I was intending to visit the village.'

'Oh.' Georgina raised an eyebrow, 'Any particular reason?'

'You could say that. I was born there.'

'You're kidding!'

Maria slowly shook her head.

'What are you looking for in Anafonitria?'

All at once Maria realised she didn't want to tell her. She wanted to see the village by herself, discover the whereabouts of her father, if possible, without disclosing it to anyone. There were dangers in digging into the past and people could get hurt emotionally or even have their lives disrupted. It was best she keep any knowledge to herself for the present.

'I'd just like to see what Anafonitria is like. Perhaps visit the monastery . . . '

'I insist you take my car if you need it.'

Maria gave her a quick hug. 'Thanks, you're a good friend.'

'Now, I'd certainly love a coffee and the outdoor café is just next to the church.'

'You're on.'

Georgina was sipping the last of her coffee a little while later. She glanced at Maria. 'Had you really not noticed George is attracted to you?'

Unprepared for the question, Maria felt her cheeks warm. 'Has he actually said anything to you?'

'No. But I am his twin, don't forget. Our feelings are in harmony, he doesn't need to tell me, I know.'

'I haven't knowingly given him any signals.'

'Perhaps like all Greek men, he doesn't need them.'

'You mean they are a hot-blooded race?'

Georgina smiled and nodded. 'That is so, yes.'

'Perhaps it's because of the sun,' Maria quipped.

'But when they commit to a woman,' Georgina continued, nodding solemnly, 'that is it.'

Maria thought about what Nikos had said about a woman needing time spent on her. A shiver ran through her. But how to make this clear without hurting his feelings would be tricky, she could see that. 'Hasn't he a local girlfriend?'

'Aaah, that is a very delicate subject,' Georgina sighed. 'Like myself, he was in an arranged marriage.'

'And now?'

'He was very stupid. There was another girl, from Athens. George met her when he was over there working for Dad. They had an affair and he wanted to marry her. But she was only leading him on . . . she wasn't committed to him at all. He was very hurt . . . '

And now it seemed he was falling for her. Maria swallowed hard. The last thing she wanted was to be the cause of any family upset.'

'George came back to Zakynthos and confessed his affair to Greta and their arranged marriage was off.' Georgina sighed again. 'It hurt Mama very badly.'

'I'm sorry,' Maria shook her head. 'I'm not looking for romance. My life in England is full and I'm satisfied to be pursuing my career.' But even though she said the words emphatically, part of her deep inside rebelled. It wasn't true. She was lying to herself. If it had been Nikos instead of George, she knew her defences would not be impregnable.

It was mid-afternoon when they arrived back at the house having spent an enjoyable leisurely trawl around the shops in Zakynthos. Both men were out.

'They're working on the mainland, I expect,' Georgina said. 'Dad has a lot of business interests over there. One of the reasons we have the plane.'

'I ought to get my stuff over to that other apartment in Zakynthos.'

'Oh no, please,' Georgina caught her arm, 'not after the super day we've spent, we get on so well. Please stay. You are comfortable here and enjoying yourself, aren't you?'

'You know I am. I'm being thoroughly spoilt.'

'Then what's your problem?'

What a leading question, Maria couldn't bring herself to answer it.

Instead she hedged, 'But what about your parents, it's their house?'

'You heard what Mama said this morning, just before they left to go on the cruise.'

Mrs Cristol had urged her to spend the whole of the holiday with them now the original accommodation wasn't able to be used.

'The middle of Zakynthos town is inconvenient for seeing turtles, you have to admit it. You would do far better to stay here. And we'd be delighted to have you,' Georgina wheedled. 'Look, while you're thinking about it, I'll pour us a cold drink. We can sit outside on the loungers in the garden under the umbrella, yes?'

'Yes.' Maria laughed. 'You're crafty. You're making me so comfortable, I'd be foolish to leave here for a scorching hot flat in town.'

Georgina grinned, 'Absolutely.' And she trotted off to fix the drinks.

Maria went through to her bedroom and dumped her shoulder bag on the bed. She drew out the one purchase made that morning, a pale silvery-blue silk scarf. It would enhance the evening dresses she had brought with her.

Georgina stretched out luxuriously on a brightly-striped lounger beneath a thatched sunshade. She waved a glass in the air, the cubes clinking invitingly in the blazing sunshine. 'Come and relax. Forget all your cares and just lie here and melt.'

'What an offer.' Maria accepted a glass of ouzo and sipped it gratefully. After the cool English summer, the heat of the sun was seductive, a golden ball against the brassy blue backdrop. She kicked off her mules and wriggled bare toes appreciatively.

'In two weeks I'll be getting married,' Georgina said dreamily.

'Can I ask you something?'

'Sure.'

'Your boyfriend, Alex, do you . . . do you love him?'

Georgina threw back her head and laughed joyously. 'But of course. I think he's fantastic. Now why did you find it difficult to ask?'

'Because,' Maria swirled cubes around in the ouzo, 'it's an arranged marriage. How can you arrange to love someone?'

'We've known each other for years, really got to know everything about each other. Love grows, you know, Maria. It's not always a flash of lightening. If it is, that sort of love very often burns bright and then goes out.'

Maria nodded. 'True.'

'I'm really happy to be marrying Alex. In fact, I can't wait.' She snuggled down on the sun lounger and sighed ecstatically. 'Mama and Dad are looking forward to it nearly as much as I am.'

'It's a good thing they'll be back in time.'

'Yes. You know, with the anniversary and fixing the date when Alex is between contracts in Athens, it was difficult. I wanted an August wedding, you see, because my birthday is next month and I'll be the same age. Silly really, but I wanted to be younger than him on my marriage certificate. Daft, isn't it?'

'A bride's allowed to choose her wedding day, for whatever reason.'

'To be honest, Alex did want to wait until next year. He is working so hard, saving money. I told him, Dad will help us out, but he didn't want to do it that way. He's proud, you see.'

Maria nodded, 'I don't blame him.'

'But after George confessed to his affair, Mama was devastated. I persuaded Alex to agree to a marriage this year. And because Alex is genuinely concerned for Mama's feelings, he has put his pride to one side and for that I love him even more.' Georgina's eyes were shining and Maria knew whether or not her marriage was arranged, Georgina was undoubtedly in love. It shone out from every pore.

'And,' Georgina continued, 'It was exactly the right decision. Mama began to perk up straight away. She's talked of nothing else for months. Except, of course, to try and pin Nikos down to when he will marry.'

It was the perfect opportunity.

'Is that likely?' Maria asked the question, dreading what the answer might be, but needing to know where she stood. She couldn't believe he would be unattached.

'Pssh,' Georgina waved a disparaging hand, 'with Nikos, it's like grasping smoke. With him always work comes first.'

Maria felt her heart lift with relief. It told her a great deal about her own feelings. Now she knew, she was free to enjoy this evening's date with him. Without a regular girlfriend, Nikos was a very eligible man.

'He's taking me out to dinner tonight.' Maria said.

'But . . . it's Saturday . . . ' Georgina stopped.

'It doesn't matter, does it? He was adamant that his time was his own.'

'Yes . . . of course . . . but wouldn't you rather go with George?'

'I have promised to have lunch with George tomorrow.'

Georgina's uncertain look vanished. 'Oh yes, so you did. You'll find him very good company.'

Maria concealed a smile. Georgina really was acting advocate. All the same, it gave her a warm feeling that Georgina and yes, Mrs Cristol too, considered her a suitable partner for George. It was nice to feel they viewed her with respect, particularly after so short an acquaintance.

Nikos was back early. 'What a lazy pair,' He plumped down on a canvas chair beside them. Georgina stirred and opened one eye.

'Siesta is allowed.'

He consulted his watch. 'At six-thirty?'

'You're joking.' Maria smothered a yawn. 'We can't have slept for so long.'

He smiled. 'Do you good. Zakynthos has got to you already.'

'But I never sleep in the afternoon at home.'

'The temperature in England doesn't reach ninety degrees though.'

'I guess not. However, if you'll both excuse me,' she scrambled to her feet and ran a hand through her tousled hair. She felt hot and sticky and decidedly unattractive. 'I simply must take a shower, wake myself up.'

7

The time on the bedside clock ticked round to ten to eight. Ready, except for her dress, even down to pearl studs in her ears and full make-up on bar lipstick, Maria stood agonising in front of the wardrobe mirror.

This was ridiculous, she'd only packed three dresses, well, three suitable for going out to dinner in, so why was she dithering? Exasperated with herself at five to eight, she snatched up the red halter-neck and slicked her lips with matching lipstick.

Grabbing her clutch bag, she hurried down the hall. Nikos broke off talking to Georgina and came forward eagerly, taking her hand.

The clock struck the hour. 'Time to be off.' He cupped her elbow in his palm and ushered her to the door. As they stepped outside, the telephone began to ring.

'Nikos,' Georgina shouted, 'do you want to answer it?'

'No,' he called back over his shoulder as they walked towards the BMW, 'whoever it is, tell them I'm out.' He opened the passenger door.

'If you're expecting a call,' Maria said, as she slid into the seat, 'I don't mind waiting.'

'But I wouldn't dream of keeping you waiting. They must ring again.' Flamboyantly, he flicked the door closed. 'You and I are going out for the evening.'

At the crossroads below Lithakia, he swung the big car to the left. 'Where are you taking me?' Maria, content to let him make the decisions, snuggled into the supple upholstery.

'Surprise time, yes?' He cast a brief glance across at her.

Maria watched the road unfold enticingly before them. 'Hmmm . . . but anywhere will be a surprise, won't it?'

He laughed, 'Yes, I suppose so.'

The evening was still very warm but

the extreme heat of the day was past now, leaving it very pleasant. They travelled in comfortable silence with the windows down, the powerful car purring smoothly along, olive groves sweeping back on either side until suddenly the road dipped down to Laganas, catching Maria unawares.

'It's surprisingly built-up.'

'As I said before, Laganas is a lively place now compared to only twenty years ago. Then, there was only a handful of houses and a bakery along the high street with a bar or two by the beach. In fact, you can still buy postcards that show the town as it used to be. All those hotels and shops,' he arched a hand, 'are new developments.'

'Which brings in thousands of tourists.'

'Yes.' Nikos followed the curving coast road to Kalamaki. 'And of course, that's why there is such concern for the future of the loggerhead turtles. All the bright lights and noise scare off the females who come ashore to lay their eggs. And those that do manage to dig nests, leave the resultant hatchlings with a major problem in getting back to the sea.'

Maria nodded. 'It's because they're phototactic, isn't it? I've been reading up about them.'

'That's right. The baby turtles should head straight for the safety of the sea after hatching, but they get very confused by the lights and often head in the wrong direction. It's heart-breaking because they get picked off so easily by predators. Their only chance of safety is to scurry down the beach into the sea as fast as possible.'

'And is this the actual beach used for nesting?'

'Down this end, yes. It's been made off-limits at night now to try and redress the problem. However, this is where we swing off away from the beach.' He spun the wheel and turned left away from Kalamaki, heading inland across the peninsula.

Maria craned her neck to read the

signpost. 'We're going towards Argassi, yes?'

'Uh-hu.' Away above them a range of hills now dominated the skyline. 'If you keep going along this road, Zakynthos town lies over there.'

'And is that where we're going?'

He chuckled, 'No, but I'm not telling you anything else.'

'It's a good job I trust you.'

He pointed through the windscreen, 'Look up there, Maria, on the hillside. Do you see?'

Maria leaned forward. 'Do you mean that blue and white church? It's got a superb belltower.'

'Yes, the church of Ag Lypios. It's a landmark. And after you see that, very soon there should be a right turn. We shall be taking that road. It leads on to the northern road across the peninsula.'

They drove on, Maria drinking in the impressive scenery, until Nikos again pointed in front. 'See, there's our turning.'

'Where will it take us?'

'To the other side of the island, the east coast, to Argassi. It has bars and tavernas all along the main road and in the evening it's booming. But we aren't stopping there.' He quirked a roguish eyebrow at her. 'I'm taking you somewhere else.' Maria laughed.

'It's definitely a good job I trust you.'

Argassi was indeed bustling and noisy and Maria was glad Nikos had other plans. Wherever it was, she hoped it would be secluded, peaceful. And, she admitted to herself, romantic.

They motored on, heading south down the coastal road, the sea glinting in the late evening sun whilst to their right, the road was bounded by verdant woodland. After the almost cosmopolitan atmosphere of Argassi, Maria found the natural beauty stunning. She wanted the drive to go on and on.

All too soon they reached the first village of Kaminia. Content to leave Nikos to indulge his own choice of venue for their dinner, she simply sat and looked out at the beach bars and restaurants, but still he drove onwards.

They passed through Porto Zoro and on through Ano Vasilikos where Nikos turned sharply left down a rough track through the woodland. It led to a small parking area where he drew up, leaving the engine running.

'This isn't what I have in mind, but I thought you'd like a quick look at the beach. I consider it one of the most beautiful on Zakynthos. Out of season, it's very quiet and natural.'

'What's it called?'

'Promise you won't laugh?'

'Why should I?'

'Well, it's called Banana Beach.' Her lips curved upwards.

'See,' he shook his head sorrowfully.

'I'm sorry,' she pressed a hand on his bare forearm. 'It's really so apt too. With the shoreline curving around the headland like that, in a golden crescent, it's remarkably similar to a banana.'

'I know I'm biased, being a native, but I much prefer it the way God intended — given back to nature and solitude.'

Maria cast a swift glance at his face before returning to look out at the shining sea lapping the sand. There was an almost sensual tenderness in his eyes as he, too, let his gaze linger on the sweep of the bay. She felt she had been privileged to see beyond his normal guard, to perceive something of the private inner man.

He so obviously held Zakynthos close to his heart and was deeply concerned with the essential qualities that made it such a mystical and bewitching island. She understood now why he had chosen the work he had. It was a giving back for all the uniqueness that the island gave to him. Maria felt her interest and respect in him deepening.

She became aware that he had placed his hand gently on top of hers where it still rested on his forearm. Simultaneously, they turned to each other, faces now only inches apart. Maria felt he must surely hear the thudding of her heart.

They remained gazing into each other's eyes, time immaterial. It was a magical moment and one Maria knew she would hold within her heart as a precious memory.

A tiny toot from behind broke the spell as a car tried to edge past and found the gap too tight.

'Time to go.' Nikos gave her hand a quick strong squeeze. 'We're blocking traffic.' Maria nodded. She felt incapable of saying anything.

Back on the main road, Nikos swept on and they by-passed another couple of developments and beaches. But slowing as they reached Porto Roma, he pulled up. Pointing out the fishing boats at anchor in the tiny harbour, he said, 'There's a taverna which goes by the same name, see, it overlooks the harbour. They serve some of the best fish dishes on the island. Well, when I say the Greeks themselves come to eat here, you can understand the quality is first class.'

'And are we eating here?'

He grinned. 'So impatient. Are you very hungry?'

'No, well, perhaps a little.'

'If you are not desperate, bear with me. I promise, you will not be disappointed.' He engaged gear and headed towards the end of the peninsula.

The sea now almost encircled the narrow band of land, a wide spread of dark water stretching away, mysterious and infinitely beautiful. Maria ran the window right down for an uninterrupted view and gazed out, sighing with pleasure.

Following the narrow road, the car curved right and soon they were driving through a sprinkling of houses.

'This is it.' Nikos turned his head and smiled with satisfaction, 'Gerakas. Just about the southernmost village, and certainly one of the prettiest on the island.'

'Gerakas is where the turtle volunteers come.'

'One of the places, yes. Access to the beach for tourists is prohibited after dusk, though. During the breeding season, that is.'

'Hmmm . . . I think I might come and visit during daylight.'

Nikos slowed down to give Maria chance to enjoy the view. 'It's truly a beautiful beach, one of the finest on Zakynthos.'

Few houses led off from the one winding road, but shortly Nikos ran the car into one wooded approach and parked the car snugly among the olive trees.

'Belongs to a business acquaintance of mine,' he said in response to Maria's questioning glance, and nodded towards the white house farther up. 'He's a decent man who won't mind if I leave the car here. On Zakynthos, you see, the island is so small you'll find a lot of people are either related or at least know of one another.'

They left the car and Nikos led her back along the road. The evening air was hot and still. Below them, as they turned and climbed a stony track, the sea murmured its way in and out of the bay leaving long trailing skeins of white lace upon the dark sands. Vying with the sound of the sea was the eternal chirping of cicadas. But the natural sounds, so much an intrinsic part of Zakynthos, far from intruding on the quiet, only emphasised the peace.

They paused where the track had widened forming almost an oval plateau. Maria looked back down the side of the steep hillside. 'Thank you so much, Nikos. Bringing me here, it's a glorious place. I'm going to remember it always.'

Nikos, too, looked far out across the bay before taking her hand. 'Do you see the island, over there?' She nodded. It sat squat and somewhat humped, lapped around by the sea. 'It's called Turtle Island.'

She glanced up at him, merriment making her eyes gleam. 'Would that be because the turtles nest there?'

With a reciprocal twinkle, he returned

her gaze, 'Now why should you ever think that?'

Their eyes met and held. The sounds of the evening faded away, leaving just the two of them, standing high upon the hillside. His arm slid around her waist, drawing her close. 'Maria,' he whispered huskily, 'I find you so very attractive.'

Leaning into him, she could feel the strength and heat of his body through the thin shirt. It was madness to believe this was other than a holiday dalliance on his part but for herself, Maria knew how very easy it would be to release the brake and take a roller-coaster ride and fall deeply in love.

But it would only be a one-way single ticket. No way would Nikos ever feel the same. Oh, doubtless, he was as skilled as all the other Greek men in romance and wooing women, but it seemed almost a national sport, nothing to be taken too seriously. Maria extricated herself gently from the secure circle of his arm. This evening was to be enjoyed to the full not to embark upon heartache.

'Food?' she murmured.

He laughed. 'And you girls say it's men who have the appetite.'

They drew level with a tiny dwelling set back within a colourful garden. Nikos glanced towards the open door. An old lady, her shoulders covered by a silk scarf, came slowly down the dusty path between the riotous flowers. She smiled a toothless broad smile and held out a scarlet hibiscus, nodding for Maria to take it.

'For me?' Maria took a lingering sniff at the velvet petals, 'Oh, what a lovely perfume . . . Do have a smell, Nikos.' Obligingly, he did so, nodding agreement.

'It is a custom Mama Carew has continued on from her own mother and probably her grandmother.'

Mama Carew dipped her head, silver strands glinting in her black hair. 'Enjoy your meal.'

'Thank you, we will,' Maria replied.

Nikos led her on higher and higher

up the hillside until the track abruptly halted in a wide courtyard where a small taverna, almost smothered with climbing vines, nestled.

Maria caught Nikos' hand, 'Look at all those bunches of grapes, why, there must be hundreds.'

'If you wish, we can choose a bunch to finish our meal and they will cut one for us.'

'Really? You couldn't get fruit any fresher.'

Nikos led her inside the taverna. 'To see what it's like,' he murmured, 'but we will eat out on the veranda, I think. That way you overlook the sea.'

'I don't believe this is happening.' Maria laughed happily. She took in the rich spicy smells and the basic simplicity of the interior with the scrubbed wooden tables and benches draped with rugs. The walls were adorned with earthenware plates and hung with woven rugs in vibrant reds, greens and yellows. Wine was being served in terracotta jugs and at the far side of the room a three-man band played a lively piece on zithers.

Nikos smiled at her delight. 'It is to your liking, yes?' Maria could only nod. 'Come, we will eat. With all these mouth-watering smells, I'm ready to try some food.'

He led her outside and they sat on the veranda drinking ouzo. Nikos raised his chunky glass, 'To an enjoyable stay on Zakynthos, and may you come back again.'

'I'll certainly go along with that,' Maria clinked her glass with his. 'This is the best holiday of my life.'

'I'm glad,' Nikos said softly, gazing at her. 'Dreams can so often go wrong and this is your especial dream, isn't it?'

She nodded, on the verge of telling him about the quest for her father. She both wanted to tell him, the urge was almost too strong to deny, and yet a sixth sense warned her to remain silent. The crucial moment, however, was resolved by the arrival of the waiter with their starter. It was superbly presented Greek salad with feta cheese and garnished lavishly with black olives.

The long drive across the island had increased their appetites and at the sight of the so tempting food, their hunger became demanding. They ate in appreciative silence and following the salad, were served piping hot mousaka.

'What would you like for dessert?'

'Well, I'm not sure, there's so much choice.' Maria wrinkled her nose in pleasurable expectation. 'How about katafi?'

It was worth waiting for, and comprised an unusual dish of pastry with nuts and honey, topped with lashings of cream.

'Oh, but that was a gorgeous meal,' Maria dabbed her lips.

'I did promise you a dinner worth coming all this way for.'

'And believe me, it was.'

'Now, how about choosing a bunch of grapes,' he waved a hand upwards where the vines hung heavy with bloom-lustred fruit.

She shook her head, 'I am spoilt for choice. You choose.'

'So easily pleased,' he smiled indulgently at her, reached up and deftly cut a perfectly-formed bunch. 'There, for you.' He placed the grapes in a dish. 'Try them, they are exquisite.'

Maria broke off a dark purple grape and popped it into her mouth. The flesh was firm with juice sweet as nectar. 'Hmmm . . . ' she closed her eyes briefly before reaching for another, 'heavenly.'

Together, they feasted on the grapes interspersed with lingering sips of ouzo whilst way below them the sea rippled in and out of the bay under the darkening sky. The peace of the evening wrapped itself around them soothing, relaxing.

They sat without speaking, content to be in each other's company as the evening folded into night.

'I hate to break the spell,' Nikos said

at last, 'but we must be getting home. It is quite a drive back to Lithakia.'

'I guess so,' Maria sighed. 'And you're so right to call it a spell. This island is pure magic.'

8

They drove back, the car effectively swallowing the miles. 'It's a good job your mother and father are away. I'd hate to think we were disturbing them.' Maria glanced at her watch. 'It's well past midnight.'

'In Greece that doesn't matter. Don't forget, we have siesta time every afternoon.'

They were approaching the cross-roads to Lithakia, but instead of turning right, Nikos drove straight on.

'Where are we going?'

'It's a beautiful night. I'm going to show you a moonlit view of Marathonisi Islet. It's something I'm sure you wouldn't want to miss.' Maria felt excitement stir, it sounded very romantic. 'It's not far, a few minutes drive. We leave the main road and drive through the olive groves belonging to Vassilis.

'His private estate leads right to the edge of the cliffs. From there you can clamber down between the lovely tamarisk trees to the beach below. Because it is only accessible this way, there are no tourists to disturb the turtles, so that makes it very special. And of course we don't advertise the fact.'

'But the estate is private, you say, won't he object?'

'No, my father's estate runs alongside so we are neighbours. And we are good friends, too.'

'I see. And will the turtles be there on the beach, tonight?' The thought filled her with a burning urgency.

'Very possible, but we'll be unable to see them from the cliff top.'

'Oh.' Her deep disappointment was invested in the one word.

'Don't be downhearted, not after such an enjoyable evening.'

Shame made her cheeks flame and she was relieved it was too dark for him to see her chagrin. 'Nikos, I'm sorry, how very ungrateful you must think me. I've had a truly wonderful evening, it's just that I'm so keen to see some loggerheads in their natural state.'

'I know you are,' he took a hand off the wheel and reached for her own, 'and I shall take you to see them as soon as I've cleared it with Vassilis. It is dangerous, you see, getting down the cliff face so he must be told in case of any accidents.'

'Of course, I'll leave it all with you. I'm so lucky to have you fighting my corner. It makes me feel very privileged.'

'I wouldn't say that.' His fingers tightened on her hand. 'You are a special person, Maria. It is I who am privileged. It's my great pleasure to make your dreams come true.'

The pressure of his hand sent delicious, tiny shock waves through her. She felt very alive, all her senses heightened. She gulped. If the touch of his hand had this much effect upon her, she dare not begin to imagine how she would cope with his kisses.

They drove on for two or three miles before Nikos pulled off the road in a dusty spot surrounded by ancient gnarled olive trees. 'Marathonisi by moonlight,' he murmured.

Maria eagerly climbed out and took his hands for in the shadows of the trees it was difficult to see where to place her feet. Nikos unerringly led her through the trees that edged the slopes of the hillside. Drawing her on to an outcrop, he placed his hands on her shoulders and turned her to face the left side of the wide bay.

With the moon high in the night sky behind them, Maria could see the islet clearly now. Surrounded by sandy beaches, Marathonisi rose up from the silvered sea with a mystical presence. It was wild and unspoilt and breathtakingly beautiful. Maria was speechless. She was seeing it as it must have looked thousands of years ago. Like Zakynthos itself, it was an island of dreams.

'I thought you'd appreciate it,' Nikos

said, his lips brushing her ear.

'Oh I do,' Maria murmured softly, 'believe it.' Both were whispering without really knowing why, except that it seemed the correct thing to do. They stayed motionless for several minutes taking in the atmosphere and it was with great regret that Maria finally followed Nikos back to the car.

They reached the crossroads and had turned to Lithakia before either spoke, then Nikos cast a swift glance across at her. 'What do you think of my island, from the little you have seen so far? Does it live up to your dreams?'

'Do you really have to ask?' Maria leaned back, her head resting on the seat, completely relaxed and pleasantly tired now.

'Probably not. My faith in Zakynthos is absolute.'

Maria laughed softly, 'I had noticed. But you cannot claim the island solely for yourself. I was born here, too.'

Nikos drew in a sharp breath. He said nothing until they reached the turn off to his father's estate and had driven a few yards down the narrow track. Then he drew up and cut the engine. 'Now,' he switched on the overhead light and swivelled round in his seat to face Maria, 'did you really say what I thought you said?' His gaze was penetrating.

'That I was born here? Yes, it's true.' Maria was beginning to regret telling him. She sensed it was deeply important to him, exactly why she couldn't even begin to guess.

He nodded gently to himself, 'So, you are one of us,' he murmured, half to himself.

'Does it matter?' Maria felt a stir of unease. 'Does it make a difference?'

'Oh yes,' he started the car engine, 'all the difference in the world.'

The house looked deserted and dark as they drew up. Nikos placed a finger beneath her chin and gently tilted her head. 'I've had a splendid evening. The venue, the meal, the company, all superb.'

'It's been wonderful for me, too.'

Nikos leaned forward his face close to hers. 'I'm so very glad I've met you, Maria.' In the darkness his features were indistinct but she could feel the warmth of his breath upon her lips and knew he was about to kiss her. Abruptly, the house door swung wide open, a blaze of light flooded out illuminating the car. His sister stood outlined in the doorway.

Hastily, Nikos sat back, reaching for the door handle, 'I didn't remember to toot. First time I've ever forgotten. Georgina must be wondering who it is.'

'You're so late,' Georgina frowned. 'I thought you'd be back much earlier.'

'I took Maria to see Marathonisi.'

'And it was magnificent in the moonlight, so romantic.'

Georgina's frown deepened. 'Perhaps you should have allowed George to show you, then,' she said slowly her eyes searching Maria's face, noting the flushed cheeks and air of elation.

'Oh do stop it, Georgina,' Nikos said huffily.

'Pardon me,' her chin jutted up, 'but this might be the time to remind you about the telephone call. You know, the one at eight o'clock? You knew it would be Anna yet you still drove away and didn't speak to her.'

'Enough of this,' his voice was harsh now, a frown darkening his face.

'Who's Anna?' Maria was looking from one to the other in bewilderment.

'Anna is the woman Nikos is going to marry.'

9

Maria, steeling herself, went through to the dining-room for breakfast. She had slept very little the previous evening and she was dreading seeing Nikos. What a fool she had been. To begin with, she had held out no hope of a committed romance between them, but in that last hour, standing overlooking Marathonisi, it had begun to seem possible.

They were sitting silently at the table half-way through breakfast when she entered. Nikos jumped to his feet.

'Maria. I want to apologise for Georgina's outburst last night.' He turned and glared at his sister who instead of returning the look appeared close to tears. Even as Maria watched, his heated anger seemed suddenly to drain away leaving on his face a look of almost pleading sympathy. The atmosphere quivered with unspoken emotion between brother and sister.

'There's no need for any apologies.' Maria sat down and helped herself to fruit and yoghurt. 'I'm an outsider, just a visitor to Zakynthos. It's none of my business.' And indeed at that moment she did feel a complete stranger intruding into a close family situation in which she had no part. 'You've shown me nothing but kindness, but I shall be leaving straight after breakfast.'

'No!' They both spoke at once.

'No, of course you cannot.' Nikos shook his head vehemently. 'You are our guest.'

'I'm sorry, but I feel I must.'

'The person leaving is me,' Nikos said, 'I am leaving immediately to go to work. So, you see there is no need for you to go.'

'Please, Maria,' Georgina's face was pale, 'if Nikos is going, stay here with me. I really want you to.' Maria hesitated. 'Do say you'll stay.'

Nikos stood up, pushing back his

chair. 'You can contact me at home, Georgina should you need to, but I'm leaving right now.' He turned to Maria. 'I shall see you before you return to England, but I'd deem it a great favour if you'd stay with my sister whilst our parents are away.'

She looked away, thinking quickly. She enjoyed Georgina's company they got on very well and had become friends.

'I'll stay.'

He turned abruptly and walked out.

'I do appreciate your staying.' Georgina leaned across the table and squeezed Maria's hand, 'and I'm sorry I hurt you by blurting that out last night.'

'But it's true, isn't it?' The slightest flicker of hope ran through Maria.

'Yes, but it was the way I said it, so in your face. I could have softened it.'

The hope dimmed and died. 'The truth often hurts, doesn't it?' Maria poured herself a coffee. She was grateful to find her hand steady.

'It's an arranged marriage, between

Anna and Nikos.'

Maria set her cup down deliberately. 'How long ago?'

'Since Anna was about sixteen, I think, around ten years.'

'But surely they wouldn't have waited that length of time.'

'Oh yes.' Georgina nodded. 'Nikos had his training to go through first. Anna's lovely, you should meet her.'

Maria could think of nothing worse. 'He said he was leaving for work, but today is Sunday.'

'Yes, he works very hard. He has a flat in Zakynthos town that he uses as a base.'

'So, this is not his only home?'

'Oh no.'

'I don't understand. When my holiday accommodation was washed out, why didn't he suggest I could stay there? Why bring me here to your parent's home?'

'Because he is man of honour. He would not compromise you by suggesting his personal flat.'

Maria found Georgina's words at variance with the new image she had formed of Nikos since last night's revelation. Conflicting thoughts tumbled around in her brain without making much sense. He was spoken for and that was that. She forced herself to look at the day ahead. 'I'm supposed to be going out to lunch with George.'

'Hmm, he is looking forward to it very much, he told me so, earlier, before we went for a swim. He'll be back soon.'

'Any idea where he might take me?'

'None at all.' She grinned. 'Flow with it.'

* * *

'You say, Maria my lovely,' George beamed at her, 'anywhere you wish to go, anywhere at all, I shall take you.'

'Well, last night I went south, so how, how about heading north?'

'Sounds fine. We'll make a complete day of it. I shall take you right to the farthest point and show you the blue caves.'

'How far is it?'

He shrugged and spread his hands expressively, 'Possibly seventy miles. But we shall make some detours because I want to show you beautiful places and interesting things.'

'And I shall pack a basket of food with wine and fruit.' Georgina jumped up and hurried off to the kitchen.

'Come with us,' Maria called after her. It would be so much less intense with three, and would certainly dispel any chances of this being classed as a date. She felt mean even suggesting it, and George's face now was a picture, but no way did she wish to give him the wrong idea.

'Absolutely not!' George's reproof was absolute.

Maria felt her knots of tension loosen and she found she was suddenly eager to see the northern part of Zakynthos. Last night had introduced her to the southern tip and she'd found the island a wonderful romantic place of great beauty.

The north was where her father had

come from, where she herself had been born. Excitement began to rise inside her, this was the main reason for her visit to the island. Perhaps today was the day she would discover the secrets from her past.

She smiled brightly at George. 'Shall we go?'

They drove north up the winding road leaving Lithakia behind.

They were rising now towards Kiliomeno and George kept up a constant informative dialogue. 'The church here,' he pointed, 'is called St Nicholas and the village was too, initially.'

They progressed on up the west coast with the scenery growing more rugged and majestic with every mile.

'I'm going to do one of those detours I told you about,' said George, as they approached Exo Hora. The road now led directly towards the coastline. He swung left again and then right at the T-junction. They passed a taverna and the winding road continued uphill all the time.

'Keep looking to your left. Tell me when you see the landmark.'

'But I don't know what I'm looking for.'

He chuckled, 'You will when you see it.'

A few moments later, Maria drew in her breath sharply. 'That has to be it.'

'I knew you'd see it before I did.'

On the top of the cliff was a white cross and as they drew closer the cross seemed to assume gigantic proportions until it towered above them. In the forecourt of a taverna overshadowed by the cross, George parked the car.

'Shall we have a walk?' He led the way along a short and stony path. 'This is the site of the Mycenaean tombs. They are cut from rock. The cross was to commemorate all the men who died in the Greek Civil War of the 1940s.'

'Did your family lose any relatives?'

He pursed his lips and nodded sadly, 'Indeed we did.' He held out a helping hand and Maria took it, following where he led across the uneven ground.

'The cliffs drop away three hundred feet to the sea just a short, distance in front. It is a place to treat with respect, I think.'

'Absolutely. But it's truly one of Zakynthos' jewels, so spectacular. That's what tourists love, isn't it, impressive scenery? And you have so much, all very varied. I couldn't begin to say what I love the most.'

He chuckled softly. 'We cater for all.' The chuckle died in his throat as he raised his hand holding hers, pointing to the 150 foot high cross. 'All those men . . . '

She glanced at his face and read history in his sombre expression. Each man lost, a person in his own right yet part of some close-knit family group. They had given all, freely, for their beloved Zakynthos. She felt humbled in the face of their bravery and the ultimate sacrifice paid.

'The member of our family, the man who died, his name was Theo Angelides.'

Shock jolted through her before her

commonsense kicked in and slowed down her racing heart. 'Who was he?' she whispered, aware that her palm, still grasping George's hand, was now unpleasantly sticky.

'My mother's uncle.'

She nodded and unobtrusively extricated her hand, rubbing it down her shorts. George turned and looked full in her face. 'You are all right, Maria?'

She nodded again, 'Perhaps a cold drink . . .'

'But of course.' He led her back towards the taverna. 'We will leave the sadness behind. Our day is for enjoyment.' A few minutes later as they sat outside under the sunshades, he raised his glass of ouzo. 'To you, Maria. Please forgive me, being a native, I forgot that you are not used to our heat. It takes a little adjustment, yes?'

She smiled over the rim of her misted glasses, 'Yes.' He was such a likeable kind-hearted man. What a great pity she could regard him only as a platonic friend. That crucial spark simply wasn't there. It had been for his elder brother, still was, she reluctantly admitted crossly before reining back her thoughts. The discovery of the existence of Theo Angelides had brought back into sharp relief the need to focus and find out about her father.

At first when George had said the name her heart had leapt wildly thinking that this could be him until cold logic had reasserted itself. Of course it couldn't be, if he had died in the early forties, she would never have been born. And the name Angelides was one frequently come across in Greece. With her emotions in turmoil, she was getting far too fanciful. She took a calming gulp of her chilled wine.

'From here I shall take you straight up to Anafonitria.' George drained his glass. He seemed to have picked up on her own thought before she could voice the question.

'Could we have a wander around the village, rather than just drive through?'

'But of course, anything you wish, it

is your day out and my pleasure to escort you.' George, his intent dark eyes flowing warmly bent to take her empty glass. 'The day is all ours.'

'Thanks, George.' Maria felt a stab of pure pleasure at being feted. She had never been treated so chivalrously before.

'No thanks needed.' He grinned. 'I'm having fun, come on, let's take the road.'

In no time it seemed the car was nosing its way into Anafonitria. The large platia was sundrenched, the heat bouncing up from the ground but edged with an enormous, welcoming shady plane tree.

'George,' Maria let down the window, 'could we stop, please?' She was quite unprepared for the wave of emotion that swept through her at first sight of the village.'

George cast a quick glance at her, narrowing his eyes. 'But of course.'

Without the sound of the engine, the quietness seemed to fall like a cushioned quilt over the car and the sleepy clustering houses. Maria sat, drinking in the atmosphere, the essence of peace that permeated this picturesque place. It was speaking in cajoling whispers to her, calling to her heart.

This was her birthplace, this the reason why she had travelled to the Greek island to satisfy the tormenting questing of her very soul. All those questions she had asked as a child, the ones never answered had only served to bank up the smouldering fire deep within her. Now, something from the core of her being sprang up, resonating with the whispers of love from Anafonitria.

George watched her closely, saying nothing, aware something of momentous importance was deeply affecting her.

Maria sat quite still, unblinking, soaking up the ambience, time had no place here. After a little while, George leaned back against his seat, closed his eyes and went to sleep, content to allow her whatever space and privacy she needed.

Maria reached the last house and stood gazing out at the wildly beautiful countryside surrounding Anafonitria. The heavily wooded-hills, with the tips of their pines reaching upward to touch the intense blue sky, stretched away towards the mountains of the north.

It had been a betrayal of George's trust to slip away leaving him sleeping peacefully, but the call of the place had been too strong to ignore. For the last hour she had explored the twisty little roads and ancient white houses bathed in glorious sunshine. Coming to the road junction, she'd been tempted to walk out as far as the monastery, but decided it was not feasible in the burning hot sun. Far better to walk at her own pace around the village slowly savouring everything and visit by car later.

Now, happily content, she wandered back to where they'd parked. George, bless him, was still asleep. She slid into the car. George stirred, muttered and woke up. He smiled sleepily across at her. 'You are OK, Maria?'

'Oh yes, very much OK.'

'You like Anafonitria, I think.'

'You think right.'

'Shall we go for a walk? You said you'd like to back at the Cross Taverna.'

'I must confess. Whilst you slept, I've been looking around.'

'If you permit, I will introduce you to a member of our family who lives here.'

'I didn't realise you had relatives here.'

He chuckled, 'On an island this small, we have relatives just about everywhere.' He led the way through the dusty roads and stopped before a tiny single-storey cottage tucked away behind a verdant explosion of greenery. An enormously plump old lady answered George's knock. She greeted them effusively, hugging first George and then Maria.

Smiling roguishly, she fired a question at George. Although she spoke in Greek, her meaning was clear. George shook his head, pulling a mock sorrowful face that had Maria laughing even as she, too, shook her head.

'All the ladies in our family are so eager to see me married,' he said. 'What they really mean, of course, is they'd love some grandchildren.'

They stayed chatting and sipping ice-cold drinks. But Maria, aware the opportunity of speaking with an old resident wouldn't come again, decided to take a risk and ask outright about her father.

'Do you remember a family who lived here called Angelides? It would be at least twenty-five years ago.'

Beady dark eyes fixed upon her face as Celandria scrutinised her. 'Hmmm, they lived here a long time before that, too.'

George looked at Maria, 'You are thinking of Uncle Theo?'

Maria gestured dismissively, 'Not really.'

'But yes, Theo lived here in Anafonitria, with his wife, you understand. His son was born here. He was a very intelligent boy. His name was Leonidas. Like Nikos, he became a marine biologist.'

Maria felt her throat constrict. 'And,' she gulped, 'was Leonidas married?'

'Yes, they had a daughter.'

The blood was now pumping so hard in Maria's head she felt quite faint, but before she could ask anything further the woman continued.

'Her name is Anna. She is betrothed to Nikos.'

Maria couldn't speak. She'd been braced to hear her own name mentioned. This made no sense.

The old lady was smiling at her, 'You haven't met Anna yet? A lovely girl, oh yes, a lovely girl.' Feeling quite weak with shock, Maria could only shake her head. 'But you must. She lives at Volimes.' She waved her hand northwards, 'Volimes is the next one. It's the largest hill village, very commercial, where the lace is made. Anna works with the lace-makers.'

'That's right,' George interrupted. 'Georgina's wedding dress is of a secret design, but Anna is making it. If you ask, I'm sure Georgina will take you with her when she goes for her last fitting in a day or two.'

With a supreme effort, Maria got a grip on her emotions. 'I'm sure she'll want to keep it a secret, brides do. You only get married once, don't you?'

Suddenly there was a tension in the air. Celandria and George exchanged a swift glance. 'It is hoped so. Now, would you like another drink?'

'No, thanks.' George dropped a hand on her shoulder, 'we must be going.'

Urgently now, trying to understand the situation, Maria said, 'Leonidas, does he live at Volimes, too?'

'Sadly, no. He was killed in a plane crash several years ago.'

Having thought there could be no worse shock, this revelation hit her in the solar plexus like a physical blow. Dead, her father was dead. This man she had never known — and now never would.

Maria took a deep shuddering

breath, needing to be out of the house, out into the fresh air and sunshine. She vaguely recalled saying goodbye and walking away through the door but everything seemed to be happening at a distance.

With enormous relief on reaching the car, Maria collapsed on to the seat and leaned her head back closing her eyes. How could she be experiencing such anguish? She didn't know what her father looked like, had never spoken to him and yet . . . The grief in her heart was a live twisting pain, his loss overwhelming.

10

'Did you have a good time?' Georgina half-turned from the stove where she was cooking the evening meal. The smell of frying garlic and herbs had a reviving effect upon Maria. Her tiredness lifted and although earlier she had felt nauseous, she now felt sharply hungry.

'Yes, we had a very full day, lots to see.'

'We visited Celandria at Anafonitria,' George said. 'She sends love and says she is looking forward to the wedding.'

'I haven't thanked you yet, George, for taking me. It's been so . . . ' Maria searched for the right word, 'revealing.'

'How about you take Maria with you to Volimes next time, Georgina? You know, show her the wedding dress, introduce her to Anna?'

'No, really, I wouldn't want to intrude.'

'What a good idea.' Georgina waved her wooden spoon enthusiastically. 'Yes, of course, you shall go with me next week.'

Seeing it was useless to protest, Maria acquiesced. Feeling a hypocrite, but not wanting to hurt Georgina's feelings, she nodded, 'I'll look forward to it.'

'The meal will be about half an hour if you want to freshen-up.

'Love to.' Maria escaped thankfully to her room. She needed a little time to herself to balance up and assimilate in private what she had been told by Celandria.

It had been a day never to be forgotten. To find her father only seconds later to be told she had lost him had been a cruel blow. How she'd managed to keep it from George was a near miracle.

Re-running Celandria's words in her mind, Maria found she was also remembering her mother's words, 'His name is . . . Leonidas.' She had seen the pain on her mother's face, seen the regret on the old lady's, and could empathise with both women. Her own pain and regret ensured that.

The following days spent exploring the island in Georgina's company were a soothing balm. The intense pain had muted leaving a residual sense of loss and low-key ache in her heart.

When they'd returned on the Thursday evening after a long day spent luxuriating upon the endless golden beach at Gerekas, Maria felt more relaxed and at peace with herself and life than she had for years. There was a healing quality in the soft air of Zakynthos and she responded to it like a flower opening to the sun.

So far, Nikos had kept his word — and his distance. George too, had been away, working in Athens.

Left to themselves, the two girls had fully abandoned all ideas of cooking meals, opting for salad and fruit when they returned. With the wide choice of restaurants and tavernas throughout the island, they'd indulged in treating themselves to meals at whichever place they'd happened to be around midday.

'Oh for a long iced drink,' Georgina stepped out of the car and flicked the door closed.

'I'll fix them,' Maria followed her into the cool interior of the old house. 'You go through and have a lounge.'

'We are being deliciously lazy,' Georgina stretched arms above her head and hastily drew back her right hand to cover an enormous yawn. 'How can you feel tired after napping on and off all afternoon?'

Maria, fixing drinks in the kitchen laughed, 'Easily.'

They spread themselves on the brightly-striped loungers and sipped the refreshing chilled drinks.

'One more day,' Georgina said, 'then my parents will be home.'

'Oh yes, I'd forgotten. They're back Saturday.'

'Which means,' Georgina pushed herself up on one elbow and turned to

Maria, 'we must go to Volimes tomorrow.'

'Why's that?' Maria swirled the ice-cubes around in her tall glass.

'Because Mama will have expected me to have had a final fitting for my wedding dress.'

They set out early next morning following the same route that George had taken on the previous Sunday. Georgina drove fast and didn't take any diversions and it seemed a swift journey, far too fast for Maria who was quaking inwardly at the thought of meeting Anna.

'Here we are,' Georgina waved a hand at the roadside displays of kilims and lace as she drove past which told of their arrival in Volimes. 'In 1988 the residents formed a Women's Agrotourism Co-operative. Now they are the centre for handmade lace and rugs. Course, there's also the traditional items like cheese and honey for sale.'

Maria nodded. If she hadn't been so apprehensive, she would have found the bustle and energy of the stall-holders fascinating. She did notice one that was decorated with some very fine embroidery and lacework. And when Georgina parked up and led her into a single storey white stone house, it soared even higher. Hanging from rods suspended from the ceiling and covering the long workbench down the centre of the room were the most exquisite lengths of delicate lacework imaginable.

A tall slender girl ducked through an archway to their left and came towards them. 'Georgina, lovely to see you.' She embraced her warmly.

'And you. How are you?'

'Very well, looking forward to the wedding.'

Maria's heart began thudding uncomfortably. Could this be Nikos' bride-to-be? The two other girls chattered happily for a minute or two, obviously good friends. Then Georgina said, 'Let me introduce you, Maria, this is Anna. Maria is our houseguest, Anna.'

'I do hope you're enjoying your visit

to Zakynthos.' Anna held out a hand smiling with pleasure. 'Nikos has told me all about you.'

'Really,' Maria shook hands, wracking her brain for a complimentary reply. 'I was very grateful to him for letting me come over in his plane.'

'He is a very generous-hearted man. Will you be able to stay for Georgina's wedding?'

On safer ground now, Maria shook her head, 'Afraid not, my holiday is up two or three days before.

Oh, what a shame.' Anna's face puckered up with genuine sympathy.

Despite herself, Maria found she was definitely warming to her. It was a strange experience rather like being caught between two strong currents. She could readily appreciate the other girl's attraction for Nikos. Anna had a lithe, perfect figure and possessed an undeniable beauty with her liquid dark eyes and elegant head carriage. What chance did she have against this girl's charisma. But it wasn't just Anna's appearance, she had a lovely personality.

'Perhaps you could come over to see us all again next year.'

'A nice thought,' Maria smiled a little ruefully, 'but I don't think so.'

'That is such a shame.'

'Well, if Maria can't be here for the wedding, at least she can see me in my wedding dress.' Georgina looked around eagerly, 'Where is it?'

'Laid out ready for you to try on.' Anna motioned her through to a separate room. 'We'll leave you to it but if you need any help, give us a call.'

While they waited, Anna busied herself in pouring out three glasses of fruit juice.

'Zakynthos is a beautiful island,' Maria accepted a glass.

'Nikos tells me your father is Greek.'

'Was.' Maria corrected absently as she wandered around the room admiring the exquisite lace. 'You are so lucky to live here.'

'Perhaps one day you may do too.'

Anna's face had an inscrutable expression.

'I can't see that happening, although it's a lovely tempting thought.'

'Life sometimes takes us by surprise.' Anna bent her head to sip the juice, but not before Maria had noted a barely suppressed faint smile curve her lips. Before Maria could reply, Georgina appeared shyly in the doorway.

'Oh!' The other two women both gasped together.

'You look absolutely wonderful,' Maria enthused.

'It fits, thank heavens.' Anna released a huge sigh of relief. 'And yes, you look fabulous.'

Georgina stepped forward gingerly and did a slow turn. 'What about at the back?'

'As good as the front.' Anna was down on her knees now, pins sprouting from a fat pincushion in her hand. 'Just a little adjustment needed on the hem . . . stand still, moment . . . there.' She stood up with satisfaction. 'It's perfect.'

'I just can't wait to be married,' Georgina's face glowed from within. An aura of pure happiness seemed to surround her. 'Do you think Mama will be pleased?'

'I hope so,' Anna said. 'I won't be on her best list if she doesn't.'

'She'll love it,' Maria said.

'Anna would still be right up there in number one spot if it looked like a sack.'

Maria felt an unwelcome twinge of jealousy in her stomach. But to be fair, this was the girl Mrs Cristol's elder son was to marry, of course she would be well-liked and approved of. If circumstances were different, Maria knew she could easily be good friends with Anna. But that stab of jealousy told her a lot. However badly Nikos had behaved towards her, she was still hopelessly in love with him.

* * *

Mrs Cristol's first words, as she leaned out of the car window, were, 'Is your dress ready? Does it fit?'

Mr Cristol chuckled, 'Let's get inside the house first, my love, before you girls start talking weddings.'

George darted forward and engulfed his mother in a massive bear hug. 'Had a good time?'

'A happy, happy time.'

'But we are glad to be home.' His father took the suitcase into the hall, 'And after the parade tomorrow, we can look forward to enjoying the wedding.'

'Get away.' Georgina laughed, 'You'll both be in floods of tears.'

'Just like a wedding in England, then,' Maria said.

'But you are still our baby, Georgina, don't forget that. Well, until you walk back down the aisle, then you are a married woman and our job is done. After that, we can concentrate upon our lives.'

The rest of the afternoon passed quickly in chattering and telling experiences of the cruise and exchanging views. Into one lull in the conversation came a single loud toot from outside. Mrs Cristol's face lit up. Seconds later, Nikos came in.

'Mama, good to see you home.' He swept her up into his arms and held her tightly. 'So very good.'

To Maria, his presence seemed to fill the room, almost suffocating her. She was so intensely aware of his masculinity she found it difficult to breathe. With a pounding heart, she returned his greeting coolly. No way she was going to allow him to guess how the sight of him affected her.

But it was obvious that everyone else had expected him and the ensuing dinner was an occasion of joke telling and laughter. Maria was included in all of it and not allowed to feel out of place in the essentially family gathering.

'You are coming with us for St Dionysios' parade, aren't you?' Nikos turned to ask her. His dark eyes held something other than a query in their depths before becoming controlled and neutral.

'Of course, Maria is coming,' George swung round on his brother.

Nikos shot him an angry look. 'Am I a mind reader?'

Where there had been a relaxed jollity around the table a prickly atmosphere had taken its place.

'I don't recall specifically saying yes,' Maria, knowing it was because of her presence, sought to defuse the situation. The last thing she wanted was to cause any family disharmony. Despite the short time she had known them, she was already fond of them all. They had a spontaneous generosity of spirit that was heart-warming. 'However,' she spoke directly to Mrs Cristol, 'if you wish me to come, I'd love to.'

The way the sight of Nikos after a few days absence had set her pulse racing was unnerving. The sheer proximity they shared at the table was sending her emotions into overdrive.

It was exquisite torture to be so close and not to reach out, wrap her arms around his strong body, hold him closely against her. But she had to deny her feelings, present an implacable front.

The following day, Sunday 24th August, they drove into Zakynthos. An air of light-hearted merrymaking permeated the whole town.

'Even if it hadn't fallen on a Sunday,' Mr Cristol explained to Maria, 'it would still have been declared a holiday. The celebrations go on all day.'

They joined the crowds of people already thronging the streets heading towards the harbour. The closer they drew to the southern end of the harbour, the more densely packed and excited the crowds became. Maria caught a glimpse now and then of the monastery and the church of Ag Dionysios, the island's patron saint.

George took hold of her arm and steadied her against the good-natured jostling mass of people. He pointed up towards the church, 'See the bell-tower, Maria, it's a copy of the one in Venice, in St Mark's Square. It's a landmark seen by everyone arriving by ferry.'

Nikos frowned. 'Maria's probably not interested in bell-towers.'

'I know she is for a fact.'

'How so?'

'Because I took her up at Anafonitria and we saw plenty on the way.'

Nikos glowered at George, his face dark with annoyance. Maria took no notice, her nervousness at being forced into Nikos' company had dissipated now with the close proximity of the other family members and the general hurly-burly. She stuck carefully to George's side, avoiding walking next to Nikos.

'It's a real carnival atmosphere, isn't it?' she enthused. 'Everyone seems intent on enjoying themselves, they look so happy.'

'And they are,' Mrs Cristol pressed her hand. 'They are pleased to celebrate a much revered man. Some believers claim he still protects Zakynthos and walks about the island performing miracles.' She increased the pressure, 'I must confess, I myself have come here before. Inside the church, to the right of the altar is a side chapel and there's a silver casket where the saint lies. I too, have asked him for a miracle.'

'And did he grant it?' Maria was enthralled.

Mrs Cristol shot a look at her husband who was frowning a little. Her face became guarded as though she regretted her confidence.

'My child, that I do not know, not yet.'

Maria, sensing her withdrawal, dropped the subject.

It was a long and happy day. A fitting finale was to be the dancing and firework display, but well before the end, Mr Cristol insisted on taking his wife home. 'We had a long journey yesterday,' he said to Georgina when she urged him to stay for the rest of the evening. 'Your Mama is tired. I shall take her back home now. I did ask Jeno to cook a meal ready for when we get home. Next year, perhaps, we shall stay to the end, but not now.'

'Are you tired, Mama?'

'I'm afraid so, Georgina, but do stay on if you wish to.'

'No, no, we will all go home together.' Looking at her mother's face, Georgina was aware how drawn she looked. 'Of course you're tired after all that travelling back. It was selfish of me suggesting staying on.'

'I'm sure father's right,' Nikos added his support. 'Besides, after dinner, I was going to suggest taking Maria down through Vassilis' estate to the private beach. Hopefully,' he looked at her intently, 'we may see some turtles come ashore and lay their eggs.'

Maria felt her stomach lurch. Throughout the day, she'd successfully avoided any contact with Nikos, keeping a safe distance mentally as well as physically as they'd all wandered around watching the magnificent parade and the displays of dancing, sitting sipping wine outside tarvenas. She'd actually congratulated herself on how well she was doing. Now, meeting his eyes, all her resolve to avoid him on any level vanished.

'You see,' Nikos continued, still hypnotically holding her gaze, 'tonight is a full moon, you certainly need that to be able to make out the turtles as they swim in from the sea.'

11

'We'll leave the vehicle here.' Nikos climbed out and came round to her side of the car. Hastily, she slid out and neatly avoided his outstretched hand. She might have agreed to this trip but any bodily contact between them would spell her downfall.

'Hey, wait.' He flicked the car alarm and followed her, 'You'll get yourself lost in these groves.'

Reluctantly slowing her steps, she acknowledged he was probably right. Now the headlights had been switched off, the darkness seemed exacerbated. It would make her out a prize idiot if she did become separated. So she waited for him.

His hand slid proprietarily under her arm and although she steeled herself not to respond to his touch, the very closeness of his body sent currents of suppressed desire running through her.

'The main thing is to take your time, place your steps carefully. The old roots underfoot can turn an ankle quite easily.' Maria gulped and nodded. Perhaps after all it was not such a bad idea to have his firm support. They walked on, deeper and deeper into the olive groves and soon the ground began falling away in front.

'Very soon now,' Nikos tightened his grip on her arm, 'we shall be clambering down the steep face of the hillside. I'm going to steer you to a wide plateau which is only about six metres above the beach. When we reach it, I want you to bend down and crawl towards the edge.'

Maria felt herself losing awareness of the closeness of him as excitement surged up within her. This was what she had dearly wanted to see and so far had had no opportunity. There were few days left now of her holiday. This was clearly the best chance she would have to see what few other people had done:

female loggerhead turtles coming up out of the sea on to the beach in searching of suitable nesting sites to deposit their eggs.

She suddenly realised how fortunate she was that Nikos had obtained permission to be here and had invited her to this closely-guarded secret beach. No way under her own steam would she have had this perfect chance.

Turning to him, she whispered, 'Nikos, I so appreciate this, I really do, thanks aren't enough.'

'Hush,' he laid a finger across her lips, his face very close to her own. 'No talking now, OK?' In the velvet darkness she nodded, eyes now searching across the wide sweep of Laganas Bay and out to the open sea where it shimmered in silver light from the full moon.

Nikos tugged her sleeve gently, 'Lie down,' he whispered, 'and wriggle forward until we are on the edge of the outcrop.'

Obediently, she slid forward on her

stomach and did as he asked. Beside her, he too was wriggling towards where the ground dropped away sharply. Reaching the very edge, his fingers bit into her arm.

'Far enough. Now we wait.' In the darkness, she could see the planes of his face reflected as the moonlight slanted down, his hand cupping his mouth muffling the sound. 'Try and lie still. It may be a long time,' he warned. 'The turtles are very shy, timid, and especially so at this particular time. Above all, they're looking for a safe place to leave their eggs where they can hatch out undisturbed.'

Maria thought of the vibrant, lively Laganas. A beautiful bay with friendly welcoming people. Holidaymakers would find it a paradise. But for the hatchlings . . . it was a minefield of danger.

She settled down to wait supporting herself on both elbows, chin in her palms. If she actually saw the turtles it would be a priceless memory to take home to England, but it was secondary to her wish not to interfere in any way or jeopardise the females' need to lay their eggs.

Of far greater importance was for the eggs to be safely buried in the soft sand so the hatchlings from this particular spot at least stood a chance of making their way back to the sea to perpetuate the life cycle.

A stillness had fallen, there was no hint of a breeze. Even the ancient olive trees seemed to be waiting. As enduring as the sea, they had seen it all happen a thousand times before.

The females swimming far out in the ocean, heavy with their precious consignment, were already on their way. They, themselves, would have hatched out on this self-same beach many years ago. Responding to age-old instinct, they were obeying the call to return but ever alert for danger, if alarmed, would simply abort their eggs in the sea.

The minutes ran into each other, stretched into an hour, into two. Nikos was motionless as the pyramids. Maria, whilst marvelling at his patience and complete absorption was feeling increasingly uncomfortable. The hard ground beneath her hip bones was unyielding and the skin on her elbows burned mercilessly. Soon, very soon, she would have to change position.

Nikos stiffened. Maria sensed rather than saw his tension. All thoughts of her bodily discomfort vanished as she raked the incoming tide to try and see what he had obviously noticed. The surface seemed empty, unchanged, just the quivering shimmer of the wide band of moonlight laying swathed across the rippling surface.

But as she strained to make out any signs, his fingers snaked along the ground, found her arm and squeezed urgently. His eyes gleamed with excitement.

And then she saw the first one: a rounded dark shape coming in amidst the waves, now submerged, now just visible as the waves ran up the beach before being sucked back to sea.

She began trembling with excitement, riveted by the tapestry being played out at the edge of the beach. The first turtle was joined by a second, third . . . the sea now held a tiny flotilla of pregnant females.

Claws biting into the damp firm sand, the first loggerhead breasted her way through the white foam and lumbered on up the beach. With slow deliberation she swung her scaly head from side to side questing about for the right nesting site. Thrusting flippers forward, she dragged herself resolutely on until she reached the soft dry sand higher up the beach. Maria held her breath, willing the turtle to find what only she knew she was looking for.

Several turtles were now lumbering up from the sea, all intent on finding that special patch of sand to convert into a nest for their eggs. It was an experience to set in amber, to hold forever. And she was experiencing it with Nikos by her side, the man she was deeply in love with. Without moving her head, she looked sideways at him and found with a shock of delight he had shifted his gaze from the turtles on the beach below and was looking at her.

Maria smiled at him, Nikos smiled back. Nothing else, no words, no touches — but it was enough. At that moment, Maria knew, although he was to marry Anna, Nikos was in love with her. Joined by their love of the natural world, she intended to enjoy the pure happiness surrounding them. And if this night were to be their only one, so be it, it was perfect.

A scuffling, sweeping sound broke the mystical invisible current linking them. Maria looked over at the beach below. The first turtle had found her spot. She was sweeping her flippers in large arcs in front. With each powerful stroke the scales covering the flippers dug deeper and deeper into the sand until she had excavated a deep pit. Resting a little after her strenuous endeavours, she then backed over the hole and proceeded to deposit her eggs.

Maria was amazed at the sheer number, but as she was about to comment, caught herself just in time. Silence was all important. Thoughtless words would carry in the still air. After the eggs were all laid, the female drew her flippers through the pile of dug out sand covering the precious eggs, refilling, smoothing over.

Then, the job completed, she slowly laboriously crawled back down the beach, slid into the sea — and swam away.

When the last turtle had returned to the water, Nikos turned to her, motioning her to crawl backwards from the edge. With every nerve and muscle screaming defiance after the enforced inactivity, she did so. Whilst she had been transfixed watching the wonder on the beach, all discomforts had been forgotten, now they flooded in with a vengeance.

Nikos nodded ruefully in silence agreement as once more back among the olive trees, they rubbed sore elbows and knees.

'Worth it though, wouldn't you agree?' he asked as he helped her back towards the car.

'You don't need me to answer that.'

He smiled, 'No. You are a fully-blooded Greek now.'

'Hmm,' she nodded, 'I feel like a native.'

'Well, I suppose you are, at least, your father is.'

'He's dead.' The words tumbled out before she could prevent them.

Nikos stopped and turned her to face him. 'How do you know?' Having begun, Maria could hardly stay silent now. Taking a deep breath, she told him everything.

His reaction was nothing like she could have expected. 'Your father was Leonides Angelides, of Anafonitria?' His eyes glittered. 'The marine biologist?'

'Yes.'

'But he is Anna's father,' he hissed.

'Yes,' Maria said miserably. 'I'm sure Celandria knows something, but she didn't say and I can't work it out.'

'Oh, I can,' his face was a mask of anger now. 'Why, oh why did you have to come back to Zakynthos now.' He spat the words out.

After the sublime intimate experience they had just shared, his shout of rage right in her face shattered her. Catching back a frightened, uncomprehending sob, she wrenched herself free from his hold and fled.

'Come back!' His shout rang out through the trees.

But Maria wanted only to put space between them. Stumbling and sobbing in the darkness, she ran on, holding out hands in front to prevent branches hitting her face, heedless of the danger underfoot. With luck holding, she headed in the right direction, and had almost reached the place where the car was parked when her foot caught a raised tree root.

Even as she cried out in pain and shock, she was thrown violently forward. Lights exploded inside her head as she hit the ground and then went out as blackness swamped her.

The next thing she remembered was feeling the movement of the car as it sped along. She was lying on the back seat covered with a rug and secured with seat belts. There was a blinding pain behind her eyes that, as she opened them fractionally, became unendurable. Swiftly closing them, she let the blackness sweep her away, but not before she had recognised it was Nikos at the wheel — and he was driving at a crazy speed.

She awoke in her own bed with Georgina bathing her forehead with cool water.

'We've been so worried about you,' Georgina bent and kissed Maria's cheek. 'Thank heavens you've come round.'

'How long have I been out?'

'About twelve hours, it's almost lunchtime.'

Maria tentatively stretched out her leg and gave a yelp of pain as her ankle stabbed ferociously.

'Don't try to move, you've a badly-sprained ankle. And concussion. Nikos drove over to fetch a doctor from Zakynthos town. The doctor ordered that you must stay in bed for forty-eight hours. And after that,' she went on relentlessly as Maria began to protest, 'after that, you have to keep your foot up for at least another two or three days.'

'I can't.'

'Oh yes you can. And you must.'

'No.' Maria struggled to sit up. 'I have to go back to England on Thursday.'

'Kiss that goodbye,' Georgina said cheerfully. 'You're here for another week at least.'

'But I can't,' Maria protested weakly, her head began throbbing unpleasantly making her feel sick.

'Don't argue. Nikos gave instructions. I'm to look after you and you're to have anything you need. He has already rung up your marine centre in England and explained you've had an accident and cannot come back until you are well again. So, you see,' she grinned getting up to fetch Maria a drink, 'it's all sorted. And look on the bright side, you'll be here now for my wedding.'

12

The walking stick was a nuisance. The church, beautifully-decorated with masses of exquisitely-perfumed flowers, was filling nicely and it would be so easy to trip someone up. Maria cast round where she could stow it.

'Please, let me help.' Nikos appeared at her side.

'I can manage, thank you.' She hurriedly laid it flat on the floor before sitting down. To her dismay, he sat down beside her. 'Wouldn't you prefer to sit next to George?' She indicated the row in front where his mother sat with George on her right awaiting the arrival of the bride.

'I'm fine just here.'

'I'm surprised. Despite having had concussion, I'm sure I remember you saying you didn't want me here on Zakynthos.'

He looked shame-faced. 'Could we leave it until after the wedding?'

'You made your feelings pretty clear when you knew who my father was.'

He frowned. 'You didn't say anything to Mama, did you?'

She sighed, 'Since you practically had a coronary begging me not to, the answer is no, I didn't. I gave you my word.'

'You'll never know how much I appreciate that.' He caught one of her hands and lifted it to his lips. 'Thank you.'

Right at that moment, Mrs Cristol turned round and saw him. Maria felt the heat of the blush that reddened her cheeks. She snatched back her hand and glared at him. 'You belong to Anna, or have you forgotten?'

The hurt in his eyes almost made her regret saying the words. Almost, but not entirely. It was true and the situation was becoming too awkward to cope with. She would be glad to return to England, forget about this man, get on with her life. She tried to ignore the little voice in her head saying, what life? Without him, life was an arid desert stretching away endlessly in front.

'Hello both,' a voice whispered and Anna slid into the seat next to Nikos followed by Celandria. Maria, having felt the situation couldn't get more difficult, realised that it just had.

'I regret we are a little late,' said Celandria, beaming at Maria, 'but of course we wouldn't miss the wedding for sacks of gold.'

'I'm probably more nervous than Georgina right now,' Anna said. 'Every-one will be looking at the dress.'

'A bride always looks radiant,' Nikos murmured soothingly.

'And Georgina is so happy to be getting married, she's bound to look gorgeous,' Maria agreed.

'She's like a sister to me, and a wedding dress means so much to a woman. I don't want to let her down.'

The music swelled.

'You won't.' Nikos said, looking over

his shoulder towards the entrance doors. 'Oh, oh, here we go.'

The wedding was a perfection of planning. Everything flowed smoothly without a single hitch. Georgina looked like a princess in her white lace dress and brought gasps of admiration from friends and family alike. There had been tears in many eyes, including Maria's, as she had pledged her love and life to Alex.

Mr Cristol, now sitting beside his wife, put a comforting arm around Mrs Cristol's shoulders and hugged her tightly, kissing her cheek. The sight of the open display of his love had choked Maria with emotion.

They were such a loving close family.

A second private party was held at the family home following the main reception. Only family members and partners were present. It was a carefree happy occasion filled with joy until Georgina waved her glass of wine in the air and announced, 'I'm not going away on honeymoon.' A shocked disbelieving silence followed her words. Mrs Cristol was immediately by her side.

'Why on earth don't you want to go, child?'

Maria had been as surprised as the rest but was close enough to Georgina to see the tiny twitch of suppressed laughter now on her lips.

'But it's obvious,' Georgina said earnestly, taking a sip of wine, 'it would mean I'd have to take off my wedding dress.' Gales of laughter broke out filling the room.

Nikos, also laughing, placed his arm around Maria's shoulders. 'You had me really worried there, Georgina. I thought we were getting rid of you.'

Maria was laughing and clapping with the others, but so very aware at the same time of Nikos' arm still resting on her shoulders. It was all so bittersweet.

She looked across at Anna who was talking animatedly to a middle-aged Greek man. What would the other girl make of it? Catching Maria's eye, Anna lifted a hand and wiggled fingers happily. It was quite obvious she didn't consider Maria a threat.

Nikos reached out to a passing waiter and handed her another glass of wine. He chinked his own glass against hers, 'Let's drink to your continued recovery.'

He was being kind now, but it left Maria confused. If he could turn on her so angrily, how could she trust him?

The party continued unabated for a further hour or more. After which, Mr Cristol accurately judging the right moment, stood up to speak. 'Ladies and gentlemen, thank you so much for coming to wish Georgina and Alex well. I am sure you have all enjoyed the day as much as Mrs Cristol and myself have. Before the party breaks up, Mrs Cristol would like to speak to you.'

Looking distinctly nervous, Mrs Cristol stood up, holding the back of a chair for support. 'What I'm about to say will shock you, no doubt.' She pressed a hand to her lips trying to compose herself. 'This is very difficult for me, but I know it has to be done.

'Because of Georgina's wedding plans and the sake of her happiness, she has been kept completely unaware of this. Alex knows and at some time during their honeymoon, he has my permission to break it to her.'

Where there had been laughter and gaiety, there was now a heavy silence in the flower-filled room.

Mrs Cristol took a deep breath and said, 'I have cancer.' There was a collective gasp of shocked disbelief. She held up a hand. 'I've been told it is a non-aggressive form with every hope of recovery. Now Georgina is safely and happily married, I shall go to Athens tomorrow to begin treatment. What the outcome will be is in God's hands.'

Maria felt as though she had swallowed all the ice from the ice bucket and it was lying cold and hard in her stomach. In the short time she had been here on the island, she had grown to love the family and to have Mrs Cristol stand up before everybody and reveal such an awful thing affected her very much.

The room filled with murmurs of sympathy but before it could escalate, Celandria rose to her feet. She took Mrs Cristol's arm and made her sit down. 'Please, everyone, please . . . she has been very brave to tell you when she could have remained silent.' The room quietened.

'Now, I too, must be brave, it is a time for secrets to be told.' Her proud black eyes swept over the gathering. 'For a long number of years now, I have been privy to a closely-held family secret. Not only myself,' she looked across at Mr Cristol and then George and Nikos. 'The men are aware of it, because they are men. They understand the drive within themselves. Women are better able to say no.'

Everybody was listening intently, no whispers were to be heard now and an uneasy feeling filled the quiet room.

'The catalyst which has brought to an end a vow of silence made over a quarter of a century ago is here with us now.' Celandria turned slowly and pointed to Maria. 'Because this girl has come to Zakynthos, it is necessary to bring this secret out into the light. Had she never returned, the secret would not have had to be revealed. And you, my dear,' she inclined her head towards Mrs Cristol, 'would have been spared the pain and disgrace.'

Maria began to tremble. She felt she was in the middle of a bad dream and unable to wake up. This was the secret Nikos had been referring to in the olive groves. He had been trying to shield his mother from finding out some unpleasant facts.

Celandria took a sip of wine to fortify herself before continuing. 'Leonidas Angelides, Theo's son, married Karsten and had a baby.' She turned to Anna, 'That baby was you, of course, my dear. But Karsten did not conceive for several years and between the time of the wedding and when you were born, Leonidas spent a lot of time abroad, in

175

England, working. Whilst there, he met Julia, an English girl.'

Maria felt her knees start to buckle and was grateful to Nikos as he, realising how she was feeling, pushed a chair under her. Celandria was obviously referring to her mother.

'Leonidas very stupidly went through a marriage ceremony in England with Julia because she was expecting his baby.' She looked compassionately at Maria. 'Leonidas returned to work temporarily in Zakynthos leaving Julia behind in England. But he returned to live with Karsten in Anafonitria and soon after, she discovered she was pregnant. Leonidas was overjoyed that at long last she was to bear him a child and he abandoned all thoughts of returning to Julia.

Maria's heart was pounding and had it been possible, she would have jumped to her feet and run out of the house, away from these ghastly revelations, but her legs would not have supported her.

Celandria continued, 'By the time

Julia realised he was not going to return to England, she was eight months gone. In a last effort to save her marriage, she still did not know that Leonidas had married her bigamously, Julia came to Zakynthos. She arrived in Anafonitria the day after Leonidas had taken Karsten away on holiday.

'Julia came to my home expecting to find him. Instead, I was forced to tell her the whole truth. As a result she went into labour. Yes,' she nodded her head very gently at Maria, 'I was the person who delivered you.'

The only thing that prevented Maria from fainting was the fact that she was already sitting down and Nikos, foreseeing how the shock would affect her, placed a glass of cold water into her shaking hands. She gulped it down.

Across the room, Mrs Cristol was in almost as bad a state with Mr Cristol and George looking after her.

Maria gathered herself with great effort. 'I can see why you were so against me being here,' she said to

Nikos. 'Believe me, if I'd known I'd never have left England.'

'Celandria is right, though,' he said gently hunkering down beside her chair. 'It's unhealthy to keep it hidden. It's time to let the truth come out into light otherwise it will blight all our lives.' He stood up and walked over to Anna taking her hand. Maria watched through a blur of tears.

'Anna and I have been keeping a secret, too. For the sake of my Mama, I have to say. When George split up with the girl he was to marry, it distressed Mama so much, I could not bear to do the same thing to her. When I knew about the cancer, it clinched my silence. We were all determined that nothing should prevent Georgina from marrying Alex.

'Anna and I agreed, privately, we should carry on the charade of still being betrothed until after the wedding to save further pain. But now,' he gave Anna a hug, 'we can drop the pretence and tell you all the truth. We shall not be getting married. In fact, Anna has already found the man she wishes to marry.'

To Maria's astonishment, the middle-aged man who had been talking to Anna earlier, stepped forward with a beaming smile and took her hand from Nikos.

'We are both sorry, Mama,' Nikos said, 'for the deceit, but — '

'You did it to spare me.' Mrs Cristol finished his sentence. 'And I am so relieved and yes, very pleased.' Nikos and Anna looked at her in surprise.

'Yes.' She nodded. 'It was worrying me quite a lot. You see, Nikos, I knew from the way you looked at Maria that you were in love with her.'

Maria caught her breath. Could it be true?

'A mother knows instinctively how her child feels. And you, Maria,' Mrs Cristol took both Maria's hands in her own. 'You are such a genuinely open and honest girl, it was quite impossible for you to hide how you feel about my son. It shines out from within you.'

Mr Cristol walked into the centre of the room. 'I think at this point, it is time to declare the party over. 'Our youngsters need sparing further embarrassment.'

There were nodded agreements, good wishes and goodbyes and a general move to the door.

Maria sat stunned, one thing dominating her thoughts. Nikos and Anna were not to be married after all. Everything else seemed unreal as though it was happening at a distance. She had traced her natural father, seen the turtles' nest and made a journey from deepest despair to the point where hope, at last, now shone like a bright star.

The future now rested upon Nikos.

⋆   ⋆   ⋆

The sailing boat rocked gently at anchor near the mouth of the cove, the current tugging at her bows. The rugged cliffs rose sharply from the pebbly beach and towered above them.

'It makes you feel so insignificant, doesn't it? The natural landscape,' Maria murmured. She was seated on the long wooden bench in the stern.

'Hmmm . . . ' Nikos was scanning the surface of the water out to sea with powerful binoculars.

'Just what are we doing here, Nikos? Are we watching for turtles?'

It was the evening following Georgina's wedding and Nikos had insisted on bringing her out in the boat. 'There's something you must see,' he'd told her enigmatically.

He'd sailed the boat expertly up the west coast almost to the top of the island. This part of Zakynthos would otherwise have been totally inaccessible to reach either by car or on foot.

Since the revelations of the previous day, Nikos appeared reserved, making no comment on his mother's opinion regarding his feelings for Maria. Taking his silence as confirmation that he was not interested in becoming romantically involved with her, Maria had also kept silent.

Once she was able to walk without the aid of a stick, which even now was lying in the bottom of the boat, she intended to fly back to England as soon as possible.

'It doesn't seem a likely place for turtles.'

'Shush.' He lowered the binoculars and came to sit beside her. 'Trust me, I promise you won't be disappointed. Now, no more talking, they are on their way.' She wanted to ask who were, but he leaned forward and kissed her softly on the lips. Effectively silenced, both by surprise and dizzying emotions, Maria sat and waited for whatever was to happen next.

Nikos handed her the binoculars and indicated the place to look. Her hands shaking a little, she lifted the glasses. For a second or two she could make nothing out and then as she looked more closely, she could see the rounded, sleek heads of several seals, diving and surfacing, coming closer towards the foot of the cliffs. Sheer delight welled up in her.

These were no ordinary grey seals, these were the extremely rare, endangered monk seals. She had dreamed one day to see what she was seeing now but knowing just how rare and so very timid they were, had held out little hope.

Transfixed, she sat watching through the binoculars for several minutes until they surfaced for the last time before diving and swimming away. With shining eyes, Maria gave the glasses back to Nikos.

'That's once of the most remarkable things I have ever experienced.'

He chuckled softly, 'I thought it would be the appropriate setting.'

'For what?' Maria was still blown away by what she'd seen.

'To ask you to marry me.'

She gazed at him speechless.

'It's a bit difficult to go down on one

knee in a rocking boat, especially one complete with walking stick, but if that's what it takes to make you say yes, I will.'

She was laughing now, filled with joy. 'I don't think that's necessary.' She held out her arms, 'Nikos, I love you.'

THE END

IN THE HEART OF LOVE

Judy Chard

Alison Ross's humdrum life is violently changed when kidnappers take her daughter, Susi, mistaking her for the granddaughter of business tycoon David Beresford, in whose offices Alison is employed. The kidnappers realise their mistake and Susi's life is in danger. Now Alison's peaceful existence in the Devon countryside becomes embroiled not only in horror, but also unexpected romance. But this is threatened by spiteful gossip concerning her innocent relationships with the two men who wish to marry her . . .